LASITHI

By

Michael Spinney

ISBN-13: 978-1544839127
ISBN-10: 154483912X

This book is dedicated to Caroline, my long-suffering wife, first reader and staunch friend.

CONTENTS

Many thanks to Dr Paul Jeffery, Norman Brittain and Iain (Sam) McLeod.

Prologue

Horror: (noun) An intense feeling of fear, shock or disgust

Some boundaries are crossed without conscious effort, slipping into sleep would be an example. In her case she was unaware of the moment when she progressed from horror to terror.

Terror: (noun) Extreme fear

The small amount of light afforded by the torch that burned on the wall was only just enough to reveal the damp slickness of the roughcast covering parts of the hewn stone, but it served to emphasise the gorge-like appearance of the passage that lay ahead. Behind her was a confusion of tunnels in which she had gradually become disorientated as she was drawn deeper into the labyrinth. It seemed an age since she had last heard a sound from any of the others. There was no comfort.

Just beyond the light and out of sight, two eyes burned in the darkness and a low rumbling confirmed the inevitability of her fate. She took two more steps, and it was at this point that all the defences of a rational mind began to desert her. She called silently upon all the deities to offer protection and even began to hope, for an irrational moment, that her mother would arrive to enfold her and smooth her overheated brow, as she had always done when she was a child. She knew that she was losing control. To call out would be pointless and yet, as if from a distance, she heard the nerve-wrenching cry of her fear, the primordial scream of the sacrifice, which indeed was her fate. She had known for a year that she was to die, she had come to understand that it was her destiny and she thought she had found acceptance, but at this moment every fibre of her being was filled with a terror that passed all human understanding. She ran. It was only a matter of time.

PART ONE

And what rough beast, its hour come round at last,
Slouches towards Bethlehem to be born?[1]
W B Yeats

implacable
ɪmˈplakəb(ə)l/
adjective
unable to be stopped; relentless.
"the implacable advance of the enemy"

Hani

Everything about the nation of Sudan is implacable. The relentless heat of the sun is implacable, the barren featureless land is implacable, the resilience of the people is implacable, the violence is implacable.

The country of Sudan is the largest in Africa and covers an area about the size of Spain. To the south

---

[1] 'The Second Coming' – see Part 15

lies the region of Darfur. In the centre are the Marrah Mountains and Khartoum, the capital, which is situated at the confluence of the White and Blue Niles. The north-west quadrant is empty adjoining the Libyan Desert, and to the north this becomes the Sahara Desert, one of the most inhospitable areas of land mass on the planet.

As a nation Sudan became an independent country in January 1956, casting off British imperialism and Egyptian oppression. The hope of its people was located in the expectation of creating an independent economy that would benefit all its citizens and result in prosperity to be shared equally among its peoples. In fact all that happened was that British colonial power was replaced by political power based in the centre and northern parts of the country. Ancient tribal rivalries were released and factional disputes soon grew into open warfare.

Following independence, a mutiny spread in the south that escalated rapidly. The resulting rebellion, the 'Anya-nya', catapulted the country into a war that lasted for seventeen years. The peace agreed in 1972 was short-lived and a second mutiny resulted in a further civil war that was continued until 2005. South Sudan was established as an independent state but the conflict between 'Nuers' and 'Dinkas' continued.

For most of its history the peoples of Sudan have only known fighting, death and destruction which have persisted, almost without interruption, until the present day. Over decades the Sudanese government have been consistently accused of perpetuating a policy of systematic support for, coordination of, and impunity from prosecution of genocide, particularly at the hands of the 'Janjaweed'.

Most of the region of Darfur is a semi-arid plain and has been in a state of humanitarian emergency since 2003. Insurgency and counter insurgency have resulted in repeated famine and the emergence of the 'Janjaweed' (man with gun on a horse) whose brutality has been unrestrained. In consequence over a million and a half people have died and a population of nearly three million displaced peoples have migrated to camps that are extremely basic and offer no protection against the militias. The international community has largely overlooked their plight.

The capital city of the Darfur region is Al Fashir with a population of just over a quarter of a million people. For centuries it was a caravan staging post for camel trains crossing the trade routes of eastern Africa. From the air the city appears table-top flat with roads set out in symmetrical grids. The earth is universally dusty and dry, an ochre colour, and is unremittingly arid and bare; it is a starkly barren land. The town has a lake and this area is relatively verdant, but mostly the landscape is unrelentingly parched and infertile. It was here, in Al Fashir, that Hani was born twenty-two years previously.

Her father, Yussef, was a trader in cloth. He was respected in the community and her mother, Aarya, was loving and cared for her two children providing them with a comfortable home. Sami, Hani's younger brother by three years, was greatly loved and in his early years was cared for by his sister. They remained affectionate as he grew older, although not in the company of his male friends.

Hani was a quick-witted and intelligent girl. It was

unusual for any child to continue their education beyond primary school as most were required to take up duties to help their fathers or mothers, but Hani was an exception. Her father and grandfather went against the old tribal traditions and decided to send her to high school and later to university. She was sent to Khartoum to live with a friend of her grandfather and attend school.

Hani became the first person in her family to gain a university degree, although during her time as a student she had not remained untouched by politics. She was pressured to join a Muslim organisation, *The United Muslim Students*, but not wishing to be political and not knowing the exact activities of the organisation, she refused to join. This small act of independence brought her name to the attention of the university authorities and when she came to apply for a teaching post life became progressively more difficult. Her rights were denied and the conditions under which she worked became unbearable for her.

Sami was nineteen years old when the Janjaweed came to Al Fashir seeking out insurgents. Sami had been outspoken about the militia and a rash comment about the 'rape of our land' was reported to the authorities by a young man who held a grudge.

Sami's family had just finished prayers and were preparing a meal when soldiers knocked on the door with the butts of their rifles.

Sami opened the door a few inches but when he realised the men were armed he tried to force it shut. The muzzle of a Kalashnikov was forced into the gap and the weight of the soldiers proved irresistible. Sami was bound and removed at gunpoint. Yussef did everything in his power to have his son released. He called upon all those who knew Sami to use their influence and to argue his innocence; a hot-headed remark certainly, punishable yes, but surely venial from such a young man.

One hot Thursday afternoon Sami was dragged into the prison square and spread-eagled on the hard ground, his wrists and ankles were tied to posts as if on a wheel. A sharpened pole was placed against his anus and then driven into the cavity of his body, tearing through his lower bowel before exiting through his stomach near the navel. The pain of having his innards ripped apart was beyond description and the waves of rolling agony continued for what seemed an age, only to be partially eclipsed by thirst beyond imagination. It was almost a day later that his body, still impaled, was taken out beyond the gate and discarded in a public place as an example with a note hung around his neck that read, 'Rapist'.

His father collected his son's mutilated body, dressed it as well as he could manage, allowed Sami's mother to kiss him one last time, and then dug his grave in a private place.

It would only be a matter of time before the revenge of the Janjaweed extended to the rest of the family and so mother and father packed a few belongings and fled to Khartoum to seek out their daughter. Their friends and neighbours agreed to sell their possessions.

Hani was living in a small apartment in Khartoum when her parents arrived to impart the horrific news of what had happened to Sami.

On the night of their arrival the three sat long into the night and discussed the future, which was bleak. Yussef explained that they had sold everything, even down to Aarya's gold wedding ring, which, with their life savings, amounted to about three thousand dollars. This should be enough for Hani to gain transport to northern Libya and then to cross the Mediterranean from where she would enter Europe and safety. Later she could send them money, enough at least to protect their future.

It took a week while arrangements were made, during which time Hani had to keep up the appearance of living a normal life. To protect Hani, Yussef refused to pay the traffickers more than half their fee of two thousand dollars. The balance was due when she contacted them from the coast of Libya and reported that she had arrived safely. Yussef had heard terrible stories of how these brutal and cruel men abandoned refugees to die. If the money was paid in full it was not in the interest of the traffickers to risk the danger of transporting dispossessed people across borders and over many thousands of kilometres. Another dead body in the desert would excite no interest at all, except among the vultures.

On the designated evening in October Hani spent her last hour in Khartoum holding hands with her parents. Aarya was distraught but trying desperately to control her emotions. Yussef was suffused with sadness and did not talk, he had become an old man in recent weeks. Hani, for her part, summoned fortitude for the parting and for what she knew was going to be a tortuous journey. At last the moment arrived and silently they went their own ways. Yussef wrapped Aarya in his arms as their daughter finally turned a corner, their last sight of her.

The modern trade in human despair is as awful as any slave trade that ever existed. It is undertaken by men who are without a shred of humanity. Human life, other than their own, has no meaning for traffickers; they are men from whom any veneer of civilisation has been stripped. No matter if their freight is male, female or child they will go to any length to evade capture, and that includes the immediate dispatch of a cargo as its value is not greater than their freedom.

Human misery is the trade of traffickers and it is often accompanied by the worst degradation of which men are capable. Women are especially vulnerable, although rape is not reserved for females alone. On any journey no woman can expect to be protected from predatory men who know the power they possess and who do not hesitate to abuse it. Cruelty and indifference to human suffering is endemic in a world where no moral code of civilised society exists.

Khartoum is the hottest city in the world, its average monthly temperature does not drop below thirty degrees Celsius and often exceeds forty during the summer months. Hani was taken to a collection centre in the middle of the night and herded into a truck with twenty-eight other poor souls, including four children, one no more than an infant. The journey began with a lurch and as the driver left Khartoum behind they headed north-west into the empty quarter.

Traffickers use a number of different routes to reach the coast of Libya, Egypt or Turkey – all are fraught with danger. Those who chose boats up the Red Sea stow the refugees away in the bilges of large ships. Small children are drugged for the duration to ensure silence; others are smothered if they pose a risk. In Istanbul these benighted people are hidden away before being smuggled in the backs of lorries to the coast. If caught the refugees are returned.

Hani's journey required crossing south of the Sahara Desert into southern Libya before travelling north, skirting the Tibesti Mountains. Then, following the southern rim of the Idhan Murzuq Desert, and south of Ghat, they were to pick up the N3 road, leading them through the iron-grey mountains. Beyond Ghat the road leads ever north with mountains to the right and sand desert to the left. After the town of

Sabha they would cross the As Sawdi Desert until finally reaching Sirte from where the coast road would take them east. After a gruelling flight from Sudan they would reach their final destination of Derna, where the second, more dangerous journey awaited, the crossing of the Mediterranean.

The easiest road to travel would have been the Trans-Sahara Highway between Khartoum and Tripoli. This is a journey of just over seven thousand kilometres which, at twelve hours driving a day, would have taken about nine days, but they would have been stopped and returned. Instead Hani and her fellow travellers faced a month-long trek in the back of a large truck with only thin canvas as a shield from the sun.

The truck had two drivers, each armed with a Kalashnikov and accompanied by an open-backed utility vehicle with four armed men and a machine gun mounted on the roof of the driver's cab. All were dressed in the robes of the desert, jellabiyas, that covered them from neck to toe and with a kaffiyeh wound around their head to protect them from the heat and sandstorms. Stops were made for prayers five times a day, an all too brief opportunity to stretch legs and take relief, although often without privacy.

As the heat went out of the sun on the first day the curious creature that was their transport, its sides festooned by the cloths containing all the passengers' belongings, drew to a halt. The truck was refuelled from an oil drum stored in a corner at the back of the truck and from a jerry can was dispensed two cups of water per person. Each adult was given a maize cake which they had to share if they were travelling with a child. Hani realised this would not be a subsistence diet and she knew that she would soon be suffering from thirst. She would be emaciated by the end of the journey and so must conserve her strength. The mothers amongst the group garnered any scraps and hoarded them to feed to the children when they cried from hunger.

As the days passed the pattern was repeated. The nights were cold and the days were lost in an interminable, relentless blur of sun, sand and discomfort. Everyone was squashed and though they took it in turns to stand and exercise muscles they were always cramped. As the truck crossed the uneven desert, and even after it joined the road, they were tossed around and it was impossible to find any comfort. The days passed slowly and in relentless succession.

If refugees are discovered by the authorities they are taken to detention centres, although in most cases the payment of a bribe by the traffickers is enough to ensure the journey continues. On the eleventh day, two days after leaving Ghat behind, the air was suddenly filled with the sound of machine gunfire. All the refugees fell to the floor and people were piled upon each other. The armed guard immediately engaged in an exchange of fire and the fighting continued sporadically until suddenly, and without warning, the aggressors sped off, seemingly outgunned. When the truck was unloaded the bodies of four travellers were discovered and dumped unceremoniously beside the road, one a child probably smothered. His parents were distraught but there was no opportunity for a burial and without further ado all were commanded to embark or be left behind. The truck moved off leaving the human remains beside the road without any dignity in death and to become carrion for the vultures already circling overhead.

Hani made friends with Dema, a young man of about her age. He explained that marauding groups would try to steal the refugees. They would then imprison them and contact their families for a ransom. More often than not a ransom would be paid, but if not chances of survival were low. Dema seemed to have heard many stories about the dangers faced by refugees and the most horrific he recounted involved a cement mixer that was pulled up by a soldier at a checkpoint. The driver stated that the mixer was empty but the soldier pulled a gun and instructed the driver to turn on the machine. Fifteen people were crushed to death.

According to Dema the most frequent cause of death was abandonment. For numerous reasons the traffickers would leave their refugees in the middle of a desert or in a mountain where the chances of being rescued were statistically not strong. Dema had been a research student until falsely accused of fraud. A friend had alerted him to his imminent arrest and he had managed to slip away before the authorities arrived. It had been his manager who was the actual perpetrator and committed the crime, but that knowledge could not save Dema. He fled and so became a refugee running from a despotic regime. He left without seeing his wife or family.

Before being forced into running for his life Dema had read about the plight of refugees. Statistics are not accurate he explained to Hani, but it is generally agreed that only about ten percent of trafficked people make it to their destination; ten percent die in the attempt and the rest either return or settle somewhere along the way doomed to poverty and exploitation.

In the following weeks two more children died as did three other adults. As before, their bodies were dumped and their loved ones were given no opportunity to bury or honour their passing. The deserts seemed endless. When the sun shone it beat down upon them like a hammer on an anvil during the day. At night the cold was a constant enemy, especially as the truck drove through mountains. When the wind blew sand it was another adversary that battered them, abrading skin and penetrating between their clothes to torment them from within. One evening they did not stop for water and by the following day thirst raged and tortured their bodies that were already low on resilience.

A desert can seem an unceasing tract of land. The danger of driving off the road is very real and so when sandstorms hit there is no choice but to stop. When the worst storms struck, days passed painfully and all were weakened by lack of food and water. Even Hani with youth and strength on her side began to be listless.

Hani always made sure that her attractive face and figure were kept hidden from the men who accompanied them. She avoided looking any in the face and when ablutions were allowed she was as discreet as possible. A camp was struck for a few hours each night. The refugees were not shackled as there was nowhere to run. The traffickers would sleep apart but most nights one or another would grab a woman and make her accompany him to a place out of sight. At first their husbands resisted but early on one angry husband had threatened a trafficker; he had been shot dead on the spot. The women always returned weeping, some had only been raped once, others were less fortunate. Hani was aware that one man they referred to as Abdul had begun to take an interest in her.

Hani had lost count of the days, the endless cycle of despair, the grind through mountains followed by eternal parched desert, the cruel diesel fumes from the exhaust that seemed to clog her lungs and result in a blinding headache, only exacerbated by the relentless sun and lack of hydration. She had long ago stopped keeping count of the days. She had resigned herself to an infinite future lying on the steel chassis of a truck whose springs had ceased to function; her head thrown against the floor with every pothole, her body shaken and surrounded by human misery. But, eventually there came a change. At first she noticed the air had a different quality, it felt lighter, there was vegetation, and then, suddenly and to her delight, she had a glimpse of the sea. She had never seen the sea outside of a magazine but she knew what it was.

She discussed the matter animatedly with Dema who said that he had overheard a conversation with their 'captors' and they were only two days' drive away from their destination. Her spirits began to soar at the thought of escaping this incarceration that had lasted for as long as she seemed to be able to remember. Dema was more pragmatic and reminded her that a worse journey awaited, but she could not be pessimistic and began to dream of being a teacher somewhere in Europe with a house, husband and family.

Without warning the truck drew up beside an old farm building that looked substantial but abandoned. Abdul pointed his rifle at her and told her to dismount. She was horrified but had no choice, she had to do as told. Abdul instructed her to walk in front of him into the house. Her mind in a whirl of confusion, she considered her options. As she walked through the door she saw there were two other men in the room, one of whom stepped up to her and bound her hands. Abdul came up behind her and undid the buttons of the long dress she wore. He pulled it down at the front until it was stopped by her bound arms. Her breasts were pert and rounded; they had not withered away into empty husks like those of many of the other women. Then, unexpectedly, she felt a line of fire cross her back. She stiffened and wanted to cry out at the pain that stung worse than anything she had known before. Again and again she was struck by a whip made of leather that cut through the skin of her back and in one place almost through to her spine. After what seemed an age the torture stopped and she fell to the ground whimpering. Another man approached her and rubbed a saline solution into the wounds. She was forced to stand and before she left the room she caught sight of a video camera in one corner.

Dema explained to her later that a film would have been made and sent to her father. He still owed half the money and this would ensure he paid promptly. The traffickers would also be demanding their fee for transporting her across the sea.

It took a further two days to complete the journey to Darnah. Gradually Hani's back was healing but she was in constant pain exacerbated by the movement of the truck and the lack of any comfort. On the second afternoon the truck drew off the road and the human cargo were transferred to covered lorries. They were told that they could not take any of their belongings and that they had to travel in complete silence. If they were stopped by any of the patrols the authorities would send them back to where they had started their journey.

It was dark when they reached the jetty where the boat that was to transport them to Greece was to dock. They were to leave that night despite the fact that the wind was blowing increasingly strongly. The weather was deteriorating. Of the original twenty-eight who started the journey twenty had survived.

Hani spent the two hours before they were due to depart wandering on the shore, at first with Dema and then by herself as she considered what was to come next. She knew that the crossing was the most dangerous stage and the one where many thousands had lost their lives. She saw a rickety Arab dhow arrive, it looked insubstantial and unlikely to withstand rough weather. There was no sign of any life jackets, but she knew it would be fatal to turn back or refuse to embark.

So intense were her reflections that she did not observe Abdul approach from behind. The first she knew of his presence was when he grabbed her and clamped his hand on her breast. She could hear that he was breathing roughly and his intention was obvious. Her thin garment was no defence as he grasped her more tightly. The moon had risen and he stood in front of her, lust thick on his face. He knew she could not run but to ensure acquiescence he placed his knife on her throat and it was clear that if she screamed or struggled he would leave her badly injured if not dead. Before she could even think of resisting he raised his grubby jellabiya and stood before her engorged. He pushed her to the ground and spread her legs. He came down on top of her and held her hands in an iron grip. Without ado he grasped one of her nipples between his teeth causing her to flinch at the pain before he pulled her dress above her waist. She tightened all her muscles in the hope that he would not be able to penetrate her, but she felt the pressure of him being exerted ever more strongly.

At the moment she resigned herself to the rape he suddenly subsided on her and she felt his weight lifeless. A moment later she was aware of the warmth of his blood that was now running over her body. She opened her eyes and kneeling beside her was a man dressed in what she was to learn later was combat gear, a Kevlar vest and balaclava. He had a gun in his hand, although she had heard no sound.

Without saying a word, the man dragged Abdul's body away and indicated to her to get up and follow him.

Hani had not noticed that two very powerful and

sleek inflatable boats were now moored along from the dhow, each with a crew of three dressed in exactly the same fashion as her saviour. In one were seven male refugees, all young and including Dema. In the other were six women, all of about her age and which she joined.

Without a word being uttered the strong men in sleek clothing efficiently slipped the moorings and the boats raced off at incredible speed and the implacable, inimical continent diminished behind her.

PART TWO

Ariadne and Thomas

Ariadne awoke one morning in November as if from a warm comforting embrace. An observer would have seen her smile, a small contented self-satisfied smile as she recalled the object of her dream; the stuff of her dreams having become a reality. He had buried into her psyche like the parasitic river worm '*Onchocerca volvulus*' that so often causes blindness in the third world, and now he dominated her thoughts to such a degree that at times her dreams and her reality seemed to merge into a complex and confusing juxtaposition, her psyche blinded by images of him. So much had changed since she had met him first, a mere two weeks earlier.

They had been introduced in the Student Union bar. "Meet Thomas," Petra had said. Petra, her childhood companion and mentor with whom Ariadne was spending a few days in London. The two of them had been friends for as long as either could remember, certainly since primary school; it was a relationship sustained through childhood and across adolescence and strengthened still further when they arrived in England together aged thirteen to board at the same school. They had been happy at Oundle in the Midlands and Ariadne was forever grateful to her alma mater for engendering in her a love of literature. Together she and Petra had loved, supported and forgiven each other, even when Petra tried to persuade Ariadne not to make what she thought would be a disastrous marriage to Dino.

On that evening in the Union bar it would have seemed surreal to predict that she would be dead, killed violently, only a few weeks later.

Ariadne's marriage vows had not been given lightly and her determination to help Dino recover from his recent debilitating drug addiction and alcoholism was sincere, despite the strain it placed upon her resilience and loyalty. On the evening she was introduced to Thomas she did not immediately entertain any thought of him other than that he was interesting and attractive, both intellectually and physically, indeed she would have responded to the suggestion of a romantic entanglement with disdain.

"Let's find somewhere more salubrious than this flea pit!" shouted Thomas above the noise, a room riven by protest songs reverberating from ancient, crate-sized, beer-stained loud speakers.

As they left the building she said, "Well Professor, this is unexpected. Petra insisted I join her to listen to your lecture on 'Quarks and Gulnon Plasma' this morning, but I understood very little and certainly never imagined I would be speaking to the great man in person by this evening."

"But Ms Minas, why is this so surprising? When I heard from Petra that her great friend and beauty was attending to listen to my lecture it was not unlikely that I would seek you out. After all I am told that you are studying for a Masters in literature which means that you are probably a romantic and therefore a foil for a logical positivist. However, I don't think that our meeting is entirely coincidental, the mischievous Petra is playing one of her games I believe. And by the way, it's Thom."

"And it's Ariadne."

A short taxi ride later they entered the relative calm and quiet of The Cork & Bottle Wine Bar in Cranbourn Street in London's Leicester Square. Their friendly and loquacious driver had dropped them at the door and although it was only raining lightly they ran for the entrance and nearly tripped down the spiral staircase leading to the cellar, where to their delight they found two seats in the domed cavern. The alcove had presumably been constructed for cool storage in some earlier time, a brick-lined catacomb located under the hustle and bustle of a London Street. The Cork & Bottle is renowned for its extensive wine list from which Thomas chose a 2005 Chablis, light, flinty and chilled.

As he talked Ariadne covertly observed his features. A slightly raised cranium was emphasised by a gently receding hairline and he allowed his light curly hair to fall to his shoulders which gave him a cavalier look. Piercingly blue, gunmetal eyes were compelling and she found herself studying him intently, so much so that she dropped her eyes in case she should offend. He obviously exercised regularly and his six-foot physique was toned, an observation confirmed when he mentioned completing the last

London Marathon in sub three hours. He talked with ease and she soon gleaned that he had been awarded a 'Chair' in Natural Sciences at Cambridge at a ridiculously young age. He was married to Angela, a mathematics schoolteacher. "That must make for exciting pillow talk?" she ruminated, turning a gentle shade of pink as she suddenly worried her thought might be audible.

Noticing she was slightly flustered he wondered if he had shown her enough attention, for she was a strikingly attractive woman. Above her two-inch stiletto black suede ankle boots her jeans clung to her long legs and the cream pullover with a roll neck and wide belt around her waist served to emphasise her bust and graceful figure. Quite tall with naturally wavy, dark brown hair cut to shoulder length, and despite carrying a couple of extra pounds, he acknowledged to himself that she was remarkably alluring, actually a very sexy woman. *Put a lid on the libido, Thomas,* he thought to himself silently.

Over the following couple of hours they came to feel increasingly relaxed and they enjoyed the other's company. Their conversation veered between the personal, historical and professional. Without intending to Ariadne found herself talking about herself and Dino, who she explained was now incarcerated in a detoxification clinic in Athens. Her hope was that he would be returned to the man she thought she had married, but who had turned into something of a monster when pursued by his demons.

She talked to Thomas about her father, the ludicrously rich 'King Minas of Crete' as the tabloid press referred to him. King because of his influence and wealth derived from a pharmaceutical product he had formulated and then manufactured from relatively early in his career; Crete because that was where his main research facility and production plant was based.

As a young pharmaceutical chemist her father, Aristotle, had created the 'magic' drug known as Myalycin, which had fulfilled its early promise. The subsequent marketing of Myalycin had seen it purchased over every counter in pharmacies around the world, its efficacy inhibiting the ageing process and extending life expectancy by an average of three to five years. Myalycin had proved a goldmine from which the Minas empire had grown.

Ariadne explained that her family had been happy, with all the world to live for until her older brother, Andro, had been killed in a scuba diving accident aged twenty-six, when she was only sixteen.

The time came to part. She to her red-brick faced, hundred and thirty square metre, impeccably appointed luxury apartment in Park Street Mayfair, purchased by her father for her exclusive use when in London, with its sumptuous two bedrooms, elegant interior and concierge. He, in contrast, to a small study bedroom in Bedford Square, just behind the British Museum, made available to him by the university for the duration of his frequent lecture tours in London. She knew that Petra would be awaiting her return and she could anticipate a third degree questioning.

In this she was correct.

"Good evening, George," she called as she swept through the lobby before being swished up to the first floor by an elevator that merely whispered its passage through space.

Afterwards she was never sure if it was that night, so early in their relationship, and snuggled under her puffed-up snow goose down duvet, that she had begun to fall in love with him, but his was the last image of which she was aware as she slipped from conscious thought into the realm of dreams. He was still there lodged in her mind when she awoke[2].

"Why physics?" He had been asked this question with monotonous regularity over the years. The answer he believed lay in the patterns, the immutable clarity of mathematics, the certainty, the transmutation of principle into hard fact, enduring adamantine and absolute. It was only in the world of notational abstracts that he felt secure, it was his safe space, or so it had always seemed to Thomas. Concepts such as spirituality and beauty and discussions of the ephemeral always made him uneasy.

"Meet Thomas," Petra had said.

A rational man who placed all his certainties within his solipsistic reasoning, he had rarely been affected by the aesthetic. In consequence he had little experience of abstractions, other than the rational, and he was therefore unprepared as he looked up to shake her hand to find himself dazzled. She stood

___
[2] Refer *Lifelonging* Part 14

beside him unmoving, in profile, her head slightly to one side and a quizzical look inviting comment. Immediately his mind began to process so intensely that words were not immediately forthcoming. In that instant he sought recourse in reason – a syllogism: *Of all the women I have ever met she is definitely the most attractive: if she is more attractive than all the others, then she is, by definition exceptional, does that make her beautiful for she seems so? ...For heaven's sake, man, speak.*

"Let's find somewhere more salubrious than this flea pit," shouted Thomas above the din.

For him the Union bar was unpleasant, noxious and noisy, infantile and febrile, an environment in which he felt uncomfortable and from where he wanted to escape.

"Where shall we go?" she asked.

He focused upon the question. "I know a small wine bar in Leicester Square, it won't take long by taxi. You must tell me about yourself and why you are in London."

As the evening progressed he listened to her, increasingly aware that he was concentrating with a surprising detachment. The logical side of his mind followed her narrative, but he was concerned that he was not engaging her in conversation. Why not? Because a noisy parallel stream of thought was plaguing him with rapid-fire questions and observations: *Her nose is not quite symmetrical, why is that so beguiling? Her lips laugh so readily and at the same time little lines crinkle around those wonderful emerald eyes. Her wavy hair frames her face perfectly. When she looks at me it is always directly and with an enchanting sincerity.*

He began to sense that time was passing in slow motion. *I am not conscious of ever having been so captivated, she is exquisite.*

She broke through his thoughts, enquiring, "Can we meet again? I have so enjoyed this evening. I am in London for another week before I go back to Oxford."

"I return to Cambridge at the beginning of next week, but what a coincidence as I am attending a symposium at Exeter College the week after that."

"Coincidences indeed. My College is Jesus, just across Turl Street from Exeter."

"In the meantime," said Thom, "I am driving out to Hertfordshire on Saturday to give a talk at Ashridge Management College. Would you like to join me? We could have lunch after I have finished and there are some lovely walks to be had in the surrounding woodlands."

They joined the M1 at Brent Cross and drove down to Hemel Hempstead from where they turned off into lesser roads increasingly enclosed by woodland and framed by the startling browns, yellows and russets of autumn. "A poem in colour," thought Ariadne aloud.

Through Potten End and on to Ashridge. Thom had borrowed a car, a classic Jaguar E type, open-topped, from his old friend Jeremy who had been an undergraduate with him at King's, a choral scholar. Jeremy lived just off the Marylebone Road.

"Tell me about Ashridge, I don't know the place," invited Ariadne.

"I have been there often and I love both the history and architecture. The building originates in the thirteenth century when it was founded as an Augustan abbey built in the Chilterns."

He reached across to the glovebox and handed her a guidebook from which she read aloud: "After generations of royal patronage, and having survived Henry VIII's dissolution of the monasteries, it was later purchased by the Duke of Bridgewater, the originator of many canals built across England. He had a palace built on the site of the abbey in the late seventeenth and early eighteenth century and it remains to this day a testament to a different and more grandiose era. The College continues to be renowned for its splendour of house and gardens, which were reputably laid out by Capability Brown. It is now owned and run as an internationally respected Management College."

"I have been invited to give an address today entitled, '*A Phenomenological model of entropy as applied to Macro Economics*' and if you want to know what that means you will have to stay awake."

They parked the car in front of the stately building and Ariadne found herself entranced by the symmetry and proportions of the erstwhile palace. From the outside she thought it both imposing and delicate, a combination of strength and artistry, and as she walked up the grand, gracious curving staircase she wanted to be a little girl again, one who believes she is the princess arriving at a grand ball.

She tucked herself away at the back of the small lecture theatre and as Thom unfolded his hypothesis she watched the faces of the distinguished, invited audience. She understood little of what was discussed, but she observed the rapt faces of the listeners as Thom developed his argument.

Before lunch she waited to congratulate him as eminent colleagues from the worlds of physics and economics queued to clarify their interpretation of his thesis. As soon as they could slip away they grabbed a light bite and then requested use of the College dressing rooms to change into their light running gear. They had agreed a run rather than a walk.

They crossed the grassed area in front of the imposing mansion at a gentle trot, she balancing on the balls of her feet, he seeming to punch his way forward. As they stretched their muscles and gained traction he watched her closely and saw that she ran with a languid, lambent grace that was elegant, like a gazelle. He, by contrast, was economical and mechanical as he drove himself over the ground, more akin to a locomotive than a dancer.

It was early afternoon but there was a definite chill, a slight mist hovered just above the grass. He led and she followed, keeping up easily, for nearly a mile as he followed the road, but then he veered off up an open path following the curtilage of a field with the woods on his right. He kept up an easy pace and they moved in companionable silence running side by side, she hoped he knew where he was leading. After a few hundred yards they turned again and this time he took a path that led them deeper into the woods and as they progressed the gloom increased, although the path was obvious, well worn by deer and small animals. They had been running for nearly three quarters of an hour when he called a halt and with their backs to a large oak, and surrounded by brown winter bracken, they slid down resting, side by side, with their knees bent and their weight on their ankles. The grass was damp and so they did not sit. Above them the oak spread its empty branches in a seemingly paternal embrace.

Having taken a few minutes to recover their breath he stood and pulled her to her feet but she lost her balance momentarily falling towards him. With some confusion he steadied her and in that moment something altered subtly between them. She felt her breathing become a little constricted and unconsciously she altered the angle of her body towards him. Curiously she was aware that her breasts seemed to swell and she sensed that he was about to move closer. She felt her pulse increase and her mouth opened as if preparing to kiss him.

Across his face flashed a mixture of emotions. He was clearly aroused but at the moment she prepared herself for him to take her in an embrace he forced himself to turn away. As he set off he turned and shouted, "Last one back buys the drinks."

It was all she could do to keep up with him until, as the light was beginning to fade, they arrived back at the College. They showered, changed and in less than twenty minutes were back in the car with the roof up and the heater turned to high for the return journey to London.

As he dropped her off at Euston to catch the tube back to Bond Street, Thom said, "By the way, Jeremy is singing in the *Messiah* with the Bach Choir tomorrow. It begins at seven-thirty in the Church of St James, Piccadilly, perhaps we could have tea beforehand. Would you like to join me? Afterwards let me take you for a bite to eat at Simpsons in the Strand, one of my favourite restaurants. You can tell me more about your family, they sound fascinating."

The following afternoon they jumped off the number 38 bus from Old Bond Street just as the rear door opened and had to cling to one another to avoid falling onto the pavement. Laughing, they turned at the same moment and found they were each staring at the other with deep earnestness. Thom took her hand and they walked through the wrought-iron gates into St James' and on through the garden to the rear which had been rejuvenated before the 2012 Games as an Olympic legacy project. This evening the Benedict Garden was illuminated by light from the stained glass window at the west end of the church. In spring white Narcissus would be found in profusion but in November there is a chill in the air and so they hurried in.

On the way to St James' they had detoured via the Royal Academy to view Pieter Brueghel the Elder's *The Fall of Icarus* on loan to the RA. This impulse had been at Ariadne's suggestion. The gallery was almost deserted and as they stood absorbing the detail of the picture, Ariadne read to Thom W H Auden's poem *Musee Des Beaux Arts*[3]. He had never found himself particularly moved by poetry, but in this context, and because she read aloud with such depth of feeling, he found himself curiously affected:

"About suffering they were never wrong, The Old Masters: how well they understood its human position."

As they left the RA Thom held out his hand and it seemed natural to Ariadne to walk along the street arm in arm. She was very comfortable in his company and enjoyed his nearness. She was beginning to realise that despite having spent only a few hours in his company, she might be in danger of letting her feelings for Thom overwhelm her obligations to Dino, who she had come to despise. For this reason she had considered carefully if she should cry off the concert and not meet Thom, but the thought had left her feeling empty. She had not considered making love with him for her orthodox upbringing made very clear the parameters of acceptable behaviour, but she was increasingly conscious that some of her feelings for him were no longer consistent with the teachings of her childhood and the mores of a respectable Greek family.

Lying in bed the previous evening she had tried to analyse her thoughts in respect of her sexuality. She had always been an obedient member of the church, but had begun to question whether the bonds of religious convention were a mechanism to exercise control over her behaviour at the expense of her personal fulfilment. As an independent woman she

---

[3] 'Musee Des Beaux Arts' – see Part 15

wanted to assert her right to self-determination, but did this line of argument make her vulnerable to a seductive moral relativism? He was, after all, a married man, and she a married woman. She was conscious, though, that her emotions were beginning to steer her into deep, uncharted water.

Equally, Thom was finding it increasingly difficult to discipline his thoughts of Ariadne as she began to occupy an increasing amount of his headspace. The voice of his upbringing told him that he should experience guilt when thinking of a woman other than Angela, his wife and the mother of his child, but the more he thought of Ariadne the more Angela seemed to diminish. The confusion he was experiencing grew out of a growing awareness that his subconscious was acquiring dominance over rational thought. Dutifully he had remembered to call Angela that morning and they had engaged in an increasingly trivial exchange about their activities. She seemed content and closed with a comment as to how much she and Little Tom loved him and how much they were looking forward to his return. He knew that by spending more time with Ariadne he was allowing himself to become increasingly compromised and reason would not come to his aid because, irrationally, thoughts of Ariadne were beginning to dominate his waking hours.

Thom and Ariadne decided to listen from the gallery which was not empty but sparsely occupied.

They sat at the front on the end of a pew near the wall and looked down on the assembled choir smartly turned out in black. Men in evening dress with bow ties and women in long dresses cut close for the younger, and more commodiously for the matrons of the choir. The singers were shuffling and stretching their legs in preparation, knowing they would be standing for much of the duration of the performance. Collectively, like a swarm of starlings, they took their places and sat just before the entrance of the soprano, tenor and bass who emerged from the back of the stage with the conductor to considerable applause.

Thom whispered, "I don't know who's singing counter-tenor tonight, but look there's Jeremy at the end of the second row on the right," and he pointed towards a cheery-looking man who fitted his dinner jacket comfortably.

Thom had always had a passion for music, especially but not exclusively, classical. From a young age he had understood that music works because of a complex combination of mathematics and physics, and he was fascinated by the way composers use notation to create sequences to form complementary combinations of sounds arranged by orchestration. He had never acknowledged that the enjoyment of listening could be an exclusively emotional response because for him interpreting music involved an ascetic intellectual interaction, which was why he enjoyed following the score to heighten the experience. On this occasion though he was unable to concentrate exclusively on the music.

During part one of the *Messiah* Ariadne relaxed and allowed the music to merge with the surroundings, it seemed to envelop her and seep into her consciousness in such a way that she began to lose any sense of time and place. She leant against Thom and without thinking their fingers entwined.

By the time of the *Hallelujah* chorus Ariadne was so captivated that she leapt to her feet with the rest of the audience and she was glowing from the heady warmth, the intoxicating rhythms and the soaring voices. The music enchanted her and with the conclusion of *I know that my Redeemer Liveth* Ariadne became aware that Thom had placed his arm protectively around her and her head was on his shoulder. The choir rose for the last time to sing and Thom whispered, "Wait for the '*Amens*'. There is a five beat rest before the last. When I die I want it to be during that fermarta with my soul ushered into Heaven by angels singing this music."

She looked at him curiously. "I thought that for such a rationalist you would be without faith," she said quietly.

"I am," he replied, "but I still want angels."

"What a dangerously romantic notion."

In the melee that followed the end of the concert they met up with Jeremy to express their appreciation. He was clearly taken with Ariadne and offered to take them for a drink with his friends from the choir, but Thom explained they had a table booked and reluctantly Jeremy wished them a good evening.

They climbed the stairs at Simpsons and their intimacy continued in the small, private room he had reserved. She ordered the smoked mackerel and watercress salad while he was content with the pan-fried scallops. A bottle of his favourite white Burgundy complemented the food ideally.

As if in a state of grace neither wanted to break the mood, but at last Ariadne whispered almost to herself, "If we had but world enough and time."

Thom leaned forward and said, "Sorry, I didn't catch that."

"It's the first line of a poem. '*If we had world enough and time*[4], but we don't, Thom. I go back up tomorrow."

She hesitated and then continued. "Since we first met, Thom, there has been a different lustre to my life. I have been distracted, but if there is something between us it has to end before it begins. You go back to Cambridge and your family and me to my dissertation in Oxford, which must be submitted before the Christmas vacation. At the beginning of the year I return to Athens and my life there. My time in England is coming to an end. I am bemused and I feel happier when with you than with anyone ever before, but it's too late for us."

"I understand and of course I respect your feelings," he said. "It's just that I would very much like to meet once more, perhaps when I'm in Oxford for the symposium I mentioned?"

"You can take me for a drink at the Turf," she said.

That night before sleep Ariadne took out her notebook and began to write[5].

---

[4] '*To His Coy Mistress*' – see Part 15
[5] Refer '*Lifelonging*' Part 14

Sixteen days later Thom crossed Turl Street opposite Jesus College chapel. The lights of the chapel shone through the window, dissipated by the slight mist. Thom had read that the entrance to the College was rebuilt in 1855 and 'is an adaptation of the original Jacobean style, with a gate-tower, a lodge, and impressively detailed chimneys, faced in golden Bath stone'. The long south front is adjacent to the Covered Market in Market Street and Ariadne had mentioned her rooms overlooked the wall that separated the College and the market.

As Thom approached the imposing wooden portal of the entrance tower he could see that the large fortress gates were shut, however a miniature doorway (reminiscent of Charles Ryder's secret entrance in *Brideshead Revisited*, Ariadne had said), was set into the steel reinforced oak frontage. It opened easily and he stepped through experiencing a quaint sensation, as if he were leaving the world behind. He sighed as he passed through the gates and was reminded of the lines he had tracked down from the poem by Andrew Marvell which she had quoted, *'Had we world enough and time'*. The image had stayed with him and now he was curiously drawn by the injunction at the end: *'Let us roll all our strength and all Our sweetness up into one ball, And tear our pleasures with rough strife Through the iron gates of life…though we cannot make our sun Stand still, yet we will make him run'*.

"Evening sir, may I assist you?" said the porter as Thom passed the lodge.

"Yes, I am looking for Ms Ariadne Minas." He couldn't bring himself to say 'Mrs Ariadne Minas'.

"A lovely young lady. Always time for a, 'Good morning or goodnight, Alan'. Staircase eight, sir, second floor, back quad."

"Thank you, Alan," said Thom as he entered the first of the College's two quads. He took the path to the right, which meant passing the chapel.

'Founded in 1571 by Queen Elizabeth the first, Jesus College Oxford has been at the centre of intellectual thought for seven hundred years. Throughout the Reformation, the age of enlightenment, the ages of steam and more recently nanotechnology, the College has been at the forefront of debate, research and progress. Like a womb it nurtures new talent', the Wikipedia entry had noted, and now one of its children, Ariadne Minas, was preparing to step into the world.

As he approached the chapel entrance he became aware of someone playing an instrument within, and the music captivated him. He stopped at the entrance and looked round the partly open door. Inside, near the altar, stood a student practising a solo piece on an oboe; she was flanked by a heavy wooden music stand that stood nearly as tall as herself. On her face was a look of concentration and rapture and she was clearly lost in the ecstasy of the music, no longer aware of her surroundings. At the moment he started to withdraw she reached the coda and as the last note faded she lowered the instrument. He could not help himself and without intending to he asked, "What is that piece of music? It's beautiful and you are playing it with such sensitivity."

She focused and smiled at him and replied, "It's an oboe concerto by Albinoni, I am glad you liked it."

"Which concerto?"

"Concerto in D, the second movement. The most perfect music to make love to," she replied ingenuously and then smiled, embarrassed as if she had shared an unbidden secret.

"Thank you," he said and retreated. It was now completely dark, cold air was hovering above the grass and lights shone from the windows of the students' rooms invitingly warm and brimming with young life.

He entered the passage connecting the first quad to the second, passing the cavernous dining room with its famous picture of Queen Elizabeth overseeing the undergraduates, and walked clockwise around the square until he arrived at staircase eight where he wound his way up the worn spiral staircase. Ariadne Minas was to be found on the second floor and as he passed the doors he searched for her name.

Ariadne was fortunate, she was never going to have to worry about money. So many of her contemporaries were struggling to pay their way through university and for some their resentment intersected with their political beliefs. Anger at a 'rapacious capitalist system' often rose to the surface at the university, but was never directed at Ariadne personally. She was popular, renowned for her friendly and fun-loving personality. Neither pretentious or ostentatious, she was understated in habit and lifestyle.

She occupied three spacious rooms comprising a study, bedroom and bathroom. Her taste in furnishings was expensive but homely. Even a superficial glance would suggest that a small fortune had been spent at John Lewis.

Thom knocked on her door which was promptly thrown open. He was unprepared for the hug with which she welcomed him. She did not kiss him but threw her arms around his neck and pulled him against her body tightly, pressing her head against the side of his. She stood back and he had another chance to appraise her. Dressed again in skin-tight jeans that hugged the contours of her waist and legs, he observed that this evening she was wearing a large, warm, cream pullover resembling those favoured by Cornish fishermen. While not close fitting his eyes were drawn inexorably, if covertly, to her breasts. He had underestimated the enormous impact she made upon him physically.

"Come in for a moment and then we'll go," she said as she disappeared into the bedroom. He stepped into her space which he observed combined feminine elegance with a practical, pragmatic arrangement of furniture. An all-encompassing, three-seater sofa was placed opposite a large workmanlike desk covered with books and papers. A small lamp illuminated the clutter and stacked against the south wall were more books that could have been organised randomly but he suspected were not. The mullioned window above was leaded and a view of the Oxford skyline was resonant of the romance of the city, the dreaming spires.

As she returned he detected a heady perfume that he did not recognise but was sure was expensive. "Chanel No. 19, before you ask." She predicted his question.

"Let's go," she said as she reached for a cashmere pashmina that she wound round her shoulders and which seemed to heighten her femininity. His long, navy blue Crombie hung nearly to his ankles and he tied it at the waist with the belt to ward off the autumnal weather. It had felt cold enough for a frost.

Stepping out through the Lodge Gate they turned left into Turl Street and then right where it joined the Broad. With the Tardis that is Blackwells on one side and the Sheldonian on the other they were soon turning right again into Cattle Street. As they passed into New College Lane, Ariadne took his arm above the elbow and tucked hers underneath, pulling them together in a tight clasp. He relaxed against her and their steps soon synchronised.

"Ah, The Bridge of Sighs," he noted as they reached Hertford College.

"A misnomer," Ariadne commented. "Actually Hertford Bridge was never intended to be a replica of the Venetian Bridge of Sighs, it bears a closer resemblance to the Rialto. But the romantic associations of the sighs of those about to die is strong and enduring."

Without warning she said, "This way," and steered him left into a passageway. 'St Helen's Passageway' the cast iron street sign on the wall stated. They had to walk even more closely to remain side by side and it was as if they were entering a maze. After a hundred yards or so they emerged into a small oasis of light, the garden of The Turf Tavern. They pushed open the door and could immediately feel the welcome in the warmth of the air that escaped. *Ship to Wreck* by Florence & The Machine was pulsating from the sound system and a young couple were moving to the beat, cuddling each other. Others stood around relaxed and talking, a very convivial scene.

Thom ordered a pint of bitter for himself and a lime and soda for Ariadne. "Shall we be brave and sit outside?" he asked. They found a niche at the far end of the small, deserted garden and settled comfortably into a large padded garden seat for two, cocooned from the cold by a gas burner that umbrellaed the small area. "This is lovely," he observed.

"Look up," she said, "and tell me what you see."

"I see the stars, the planets, the nebulae. I perceive the perfect precision of a universe working with clockwork accuracy according to the immutable laws of nature. It is beautiful."

"And beyond the stars?"

"Nothing."

"Are you sure? That beauty you mention, is it only to be found in rational explanations or is it possible an aesthetic exists that connects you with something you don't understand but have the capacity to appreciate? Something beyond the stars?"

"Maybe, but if it is beyond my understanding it is not empirical. Reality is observable and so that's where I put my faith, not in an intangible."

"We must always look beyond the stars if we are to follow our dreams," Ariadne said softly.

He took her hand.

"Be careful," she whispered, "don't tread on my dreams."

The door to the bar opened and the strains of Bruce Springsteen singing *Dream Baby Dream* drifted out to them melodiously at that moment.

"I don't follow what you're saying," Thom said.

"There's a poem by W B Yeats, *The Cloths of Heaven,*" and she recited for him,

> *'Had I the heaven's embroidered cloths,*
> *Enwrought with golden and silver light,*
> *The blue and the dim and the dark cloths*
> *Of night and light and the half-light;*
> *I would spread the cloths under your feet:*
> *But I, being poor, have only my dreams;*
> *I have spread my dreams under your feet;*
> *Tread softly because you tread on my dream.'*

"Thom, I have thought long and hard about our time together. Just for tonight I want you to be mine. It is impossible to know what might have been, a future for us will only ever be a dream, but please tread softly so that our dream can sustain me in the months and years to come."

He was unsure exactly what she was saying to him, but he thought that maybe she was communicating what he had come to understand about his own feelings for her, that he was faced with an irresistible force. To cover his confusion and to avoid the mood becoming melancholic he said, "Tell me about your family."

"Well. In brief. My father made a fortune as a young man when he patented a drug he had created, Myalycin. He met and married after a whirlwind romance. Gina, my mother, is reputed to have been a great beauty, although you would not know it now if you were to meet her today. She was broken by the tragedy of my brother's death. He was ten years older than me and after I was born they seemed a blessed couple who moved in the most influential of Athenian society. They were feted and all doors were open to them. My father accumulated ever greater influence and wealth and they were happy.

"The only other really unhappy event that took place in their lives happened before I was born, when father's business partner and wife were killed on their way home one night. Their car left the road high up in the mountains of Crete when they were travelling home back to the coast to collect their son, Dino, who was staying with my parents. Dino was adopted by my parents. He is ten years older than me and so the same age as my brother, Andro, who would be thirty-six now were he alive. My father had brought both boys into the business and his dream was to be able to hand over to them in time. To be honest Dino was the more interested and capable of the two, but the expectation was that they would share in the future of the company. That was until tragedy struck when I was sixteen.

"Andro had a passion for deep sea diving. One day when swimming offshore around an old wreck at fifty metres the first of his aqualung tanks emptied and so he switched to his reserve. The coroner said it was a tragic accident because the second tank had been fatally filled with nitrogen.

"The happy, loving mother I had known slipped into a world of grief and one day fell on the grand staircase of our house. She broke her back in two places and has been confined to a wheelchair ever since. The accident, combined with the experience of losing her beloved son, eventually brought on premature dementia. She has never walked since and for the last two years has been locked away in a special care unit."

"Good heavens," commented Thom. "Go on."

"Much of my father's love and paternal energy began to be focused on Dino. After the awfulness of Andro's death I returned to school in England, but after A levels I wanted to go home to Greece. I was in a very confused state of mind.

"Dino is very intelligent and had followed in my father's footsteps as a bio-chemist. Dino has been working upon a second generation Myalycin and as I understand it the company is near to patenting it, and it will make them even richer. However, at the time I returned, the Euro crisis was beginning to lap at the roots of the economy and increasingly Dino was being given responsibility for running aspects of the company and for diversification of their business interests. Despite what was happening to the country he was becoming a rich and influential man in his own right and he was leading the life of a wealthy and powerful international entrepreneur.

"From the moment I returned home aged eighteen Dino focused his enormous charm upon me and I had never before experienced anything to match the attention or intensity. By the time I was twenty we were married and everyone predicted a golden future. The Minas dynasty was set to continue.

"But I had not seen the shadow that I now perceive in Dino's soul, and his erratic behaviour began to corrupt our relationship. His reliance on alcohol and cocaine became more habitual and it changed his nature. He became increasingly abusive and sometimes violent. Just over four years ago his doctors recommended an extended stay in a clinic where he has been a regular ever since. I decided that I would return to England as an undergraduate and now you find me completing my MPhil. In fact, as I told you, my dissertation is due to be submitted in a couple of weeks. That's it."

It was as though the darkness had sequestered them and they were alone; unconsciously they had moved closer on the bench. As Ariadne had been relating her story her hand had strayed onto Thom's knee and unconsciously it had moved to his inner thigh to keep warm. Now they were suddenly very aware of each other again and there was an intensity to their gaze, it was as if each were giving and receiving the confirmation they sought without having to speak, the intimacy was palpable.

"And so where does that leave you and Dino, now?"

"I will return to Athens, to my gilded cage. It is my duty and destiny. I shall depart soon after I leave Oxford, probably in mid-December."

The mood had become subdued and the cold was beginning to penetrate.

As they walked quickly back down the alley he pulled her closer and they merged into the shadows. Neither was aware of another silhouette, one that flitted behind silently matching their steps but at a distance.

As they passed the Sheldonian they paused to listen to the wonderful harmony that emanated; it captivated them. Two violins were playing the Bach double concerto and the instruments intertwined to weave a pattern.

"The violins are like two butterflies flying in perfect tandem twisting and turning, it's as if they are making love on the wing," mused Thom.

The secret door into the College welcomed their return. Ice had formed on the grass and the frost glistened in the light of a full moon in a cloudless sky.

She was embraced by a mist into which her whole being was subsumed.

Barely conscious but entirely aware of her surroundings she realised that she was moving rhythmically, a sentient iambic pentameter as he dextrously coaxed her across the waves of successive orgasms.

But this time it was different because he had joined her on the journey. Her nipples brushed his chest with acute sensitivity as their embrace began to tighten and their mutual absorption moved to yet another pitch. It was as if a special key to her body were being wound and she tensed further sensing that the moment of release was approaching. Deep inside him a tremor began. He held back for as long as possible, but her vaginal grip on him was tightening and all control was abandoned as a wave gathered them and took them crashing to the shore.

Later their lovemaking became less urgent, as they adapted to each other's needs, but also more desperate as both were aware that the hours were running away from them ever more quickly.

With dawn a sadness crept into their lovemaking. They clung to each other until at last Ariadne broke the spell.

"You know, don't you, that our time has run out? We may not communicate again or live in hope of a meeting in some future place or at some future time.

"I love you Thom, with all my soul I love you. Treasure what we have had."

She slipped out of bed and he could hear her showering. He dressed and closed the door silently as he left.

Later she would write the poem, Oxford[6].

---

[6] Refer *Lifelonging* Part 14

It had seemed so natural. As they walked his hand had slipped under her pullover and settled on the waist of her jeans warmed by the smooth flesh of her lower back. Back in College they started to ascend the staircase and he was just behind her when she caught her foot on a step, and at that moment he could not help placing his hand softly on the perfect spherical roundness of her bottom encased in jeans like a second skin. She turned and his vision filled with the nearness of her.

Closing the door to her room she drew him towards her as she slipped off her pashmina and pulled up her jumper. With the ease of long practice her hand wound round her back and unclipped her bra. He could hardly breathe. Her perfectly shaped upper body supported breasts full and round. His lips nuzzled her sensitive nipples and as he gave her a little nip she squealed with pleasure. He felt her begin to slip his coat down his back and they had to break for a moment to free his arms. He took a step back to study her in more detail and as he did so she undid her waist button and then her zip revealing a small triangle of pure white silk. His hand gently slid between her legs and as his fingers passed across her pubis she gave a little shiver of excitement. She stepped out of her shoes, lowered her trousers which pulled down her pants, she balanced against his shoulder as one leg after another slipped from their glove-like restraint.

She stretched and stood tall, then she began to

undress him until he stood before her muscular and proud, his hair falling to his shoulders. She took his head between her hands and their kiss was seductive and passionate, their bodies touching. He slid his hands down her back and it was as if her skin had become electric to his touch.

He guided her to the edge of the bed and knelt before her. She lay back and her whole body spasmed as his tongue forcefully but gently sought her hidden recesses. She wanted more, she yearned for more, and she pulled him up to face her on the pillow, it was then that they had merged as one.

The rest of that day she lived as if numb of all feeling. She was booked to visit 'Dumbledore' the nickname she gave to her tutor, Professor Lewis. They were due to discuss some minor amendments to her dissertation which was ready for imminent submission. The meeting was not a success as she was distracted, losing focus and unable to follow what he was saying. In the end he suggested they meet again the following day.

On the way back to her staircase she popped into the Porter's Lodge to pick up any messages.

"Hello Alan," she said. "Do you have anything for me?"

"Oh yes, miss, I have a letter, it was delivered by hand." He passed a large A4 envelope over the counter and the handwriting was bold, confident and a little on the large size written in brown ink.

She could not help herself from hurrying back to her rooms where she practically tore open the envelope, withdrawing a single sheet of paper.

'I LOVE YOU THOM'
you said

Three words,
inconsequential,
but

By you uttered,
the progenitor
of a Super Nova,

Engender in me
an explosion of
cosmic proportion.

What matters coils
into a density,
a mass unsustainable

Triggered by those words
That grant me
supremacy

To roam
The heavens,
a celestial king
newly born.

Ariadne had completed her time at Oxford, handed back the keys to her rooms and agreed to sell the furniture at a highly preferential rate. She had packed all her bits and pieces which were to be transported separately back to the flat in London. These included all her books with which she could not bring herself to part. It was with a tangible sense of sadness that she wished Alan all the best for the future.

The evening before she had arranged a party with friends to 'celebrate' the completion and submission of her magnum opus. It had been a lively affair and much enjoyed by all but her. Her father had emailed to say how proud he was of her and asked when she would fly back to Athens.

The despondency that continued to enshroud her was like an Oxford autumnal mist that would not shift. She had heard nothing further from Thom as per their pact.

She boarded the Oxford Express from Gloucester Green at 15.20, and duly arrived at Victoria an hour and a half later. She was returning to the flat she shared with Petra.

She decided to walk to Park Street and on an

impulse deviated to Brook Street where she popped into number 25, '*Aspinal of London*'. She cheered herself by purchasing a handbag, the capacious *Marylebone Tote in Pegasus Ivory Print*. The soft material and lovely design made her feel feminine and in control. The £850.00 price tag was excessive but she was financially independent, for her father had settled an extremely large Trust upon her from which she could draw at any time, and today she needed cheering up.

However, the pleasure she gained from her purchase was only a distraction from the sadness that accompanied her like a shadow. Thom would by now be back with his family and had probably rationalised their time together as a deviation from his purpose as husband, father and scientist.

As she passed the restaurant 'Le Gavroche' she approached the apartment in Park Street and all seemed as it had when she left. Her father allowed Petra to share the flat as a permanent resident.

She crossed the hall, greeted the concierge, George, and was swept upwards in the elevator. By now it was dark outside. She unlocked the door and noticed a pile of post addressed to her on the table to the right of the door. She called a greeting to Petra and there was a muffled reply from the bathroom.

She dropped her bag and carried the letters placing them at the far end of the solid mahogany dining room table with the hardback book that she was reading, '*Where Angels Fear To Tread*' by E M Forster. She crossed the room and foraged in the top left-hand drawer of the desk for a letter opener. She then sat on one of the carver chairs to read her post. As she sifted disinterestedly through the pile her hand was arrested by an envelope addressed in brown ink, her name and address written in a large and firm hand. Breathlessly, she sat, slit open the envelope and withdrew a single sheet of paper.

About suffering they were never wrong.

THE NATURE OF LOVE

Like lovers clasped in irons the planets and time
Bind each close with captive band, adamantine.
From north to south, like magnets to the poles,
Earth and Moon dance intricate steps, souls,
Locked like atoms in an embrace that can't be broken,
Are bound apart in one another's arms, love unspoken.
Held by a force stronger than their nativity
Endlessly, orbiting in the other's gravity.

So the nature of love and the lover imitate the stars' passion;
Cannot draw apart, fused and compelled by their attraction,
They form a universal perfection bound in perpetual motion.
And, as it is that we perceive an object in its reflection,
Your love is mirrored by the devotion you see in me,
Which is the compulsion of love, the love I feel for thee.

He had written her a poem, a sonnet. She was so caught up in confusion and reverie that she did not hear the sash window to the fire escape slide sibilantly open and she was blissfully unaware of a menacing presence behind her until she felt a hand upon her shoulder. At that moment all colour drained from her face.

Petra had been washing her hair, humming to herself and planning her evening out with Ariadne. She needed to catch up with all that had happened in Oxford. She knew momentous events had taken place but, as yet, she had no detail. Perhaps, just perhaps an enduring love might be developing, although Ariadne's loyalty to Dino was her Achilles heel because the two of them would never be happy.

The assassin drew a cruel knife from his belt, no more than six inches long but surgically sharp and fashioned to inflict death. He cradled his hand around Ariadne's mouth and pulled her neck taut. He nicked the skin just above the jugular and was about to drive his hand down with full force when he heard the handle of the door behind him turn. He whipped around and in one fluid reflex movement threw the knife with unerring accuracy. With her right hand holding a towel around her head and her left gripping another wrapped around her body Petra was unable to deflect the object flying towards her. It probably would have been in vain anyway.

In that adrenaline-fueled moment all of Ariadne's reaction to the threat she faced combined with her instinct for survival. She lifted the chair and drove it downwards, pinioning the assassin's right foot and incapacitating him temporarily. The unexpected had the desired effect and gave her the time and opportunity to reach for the book which she drove in a chopping movement into the man's throat, breaking the hyoid bone, causing him to release her and grasp his neck. As he bent forward she grabbed the letter opener from the table beside her with her right hand and with all her force rammed it over her left shoulder fortuitously finding his eye socket. She pushed with all her force until the hilt was embedded. Behind the eye lies the frontal lobe of the brain and the depth of penetration ensured that the man died on his feet. He fell to the floor with a sigh.

Ariadne's first thought was to push the flat's panic button and then she turned and saw Petra. All she could manage was to cradle her dying friend and wait as gradually the luminosity of her eyes dimmed and her blood pumped more slowly across the thickly piled carpet. On arrival this was how the armed response team found them, Ariadne supporting Petra locked in an embrace.

PART THREE

Thom

Following the symposium in Oxford Thom had returned to London to fulfil his obligations at University College, but now he was free to return home to Cambridge and he was longing to see Little Tom who he knew had missed him greatly. He would not inflict hurt upon his devoted wife and loving son and his brief fascination with Ariadne could not have continued, it had to end, he knew that. In fact, he had never before been unfaithful to Angela and he was proud of being a family man who took his responsibilities seriously.

Thom packed his few essentials in a rucksack and left the keys to the flat the university had made available for him on a table. He decided that as it was such a splendid late autumn English day he would walk from Bedford Square to King's Cross.

The railings around the square created the impression of a safe space and young children's voices could be heard squealing as they chased each other around the grass and in and out of the trees. Their mothers sat, relaxed, chatting amongst themselves and passing the early afternoon in calm and relaxation. At the Euston Road he turned right, passed the British Library and then on to St Pancras station before turning left into the voluminous cavern of King's Cross. He waited patiently for the display board to announce the departure before walking to platform seven from where the 15.05 would leave for Cambridge getting him home by about five o'clock he hoped.

December had arrived and it was nearly three weeks since he and Ariadne had plumbed the depth of their feelings for one another and he continued to be utterly bewildered by what had happened. He had always been devoted to Angela but now the basis of so many of his certainties had been challenged. While he knew that whatever had passed between him and Ariadne was in the past he was unable to rationalise the events that had taken place, disconcerting for a man who elevated reason above all else. His mind was in constant turmoil; he was aware that some profound shift had taken place in his psyche which it would be necessary to suppress but impossible to overturn. What had happened was over, so why did a prevailing sense persist that he would never be able to wade back to the shore of simple devotion? Ariadne would always be waving from the edge of his memory, like some character from a Greek myth, perpetually lodged in his consciousness.

As he was passing a newsagent the lurid headline from a daily paper shouted the story of the murder of a woman in a prominent part of Mayfair. He only gave the article a cursory look before buying the paper, lodging it in his coat pocket and hurrying to board his train. He was pleased that he had managed to upgrade to first class for a mere ten pounds and he settled comfortably into the reserved seat. A hostess poured him a cup of coffee and he relaxed, looking forward to the journey. He had been away too long. Then he took out the paper and started to read more attentively.

The name Ariadne Minas and murder seared into his vision. Desperately he sought detail and it took a few minutes before he grasped the order of events, it was Petra who had died, but Ariadne had been there with her friend. The police were saying that the murderer was probably a burglar who had been disturbed, at least this was the interpretation they were giving to the press. It seemed that Ariadne had managed to save her own life but not Petra's. He scoured the article for every little detail he could glean.

Gradually his violently vacillating emotions began to come under control. *Analyse*, he told himself. *Petra is dead but Ariadne is alive. This was a random act, or it was deliberately targeted? If deliberate then of the two women, which is the more likely to be a chosen victim? If Ariadne, then who could be behind the attempt on her life and, more pertinently, why?*

The questions were unanswerable. What should he do? He could not go to Ariadne and might in fact place her in greater danger if he appeared out of nowhere as her lover. She had been absolutely clear. "*You know don't you that our time has run out? We may not communicate again or live in hope of a meeting in some future place or at some future time.*" He could hear her words with absolute clarity.

The rest of the journey passed in an uproar of confusion, but as the train slowed into Cambridge station he knew the only decision to take was not to communicate with her, even an email might be compromising. He would though, somehow, send her a message so that she knew he was aware of her predicament, her pain and her loss.

From the terminus he walked along Station Road across Hills Road, down past the Sainsbury Laboratory, finally arriving at number 11 Pemberton Terrace, the three bedroomed, comfortable, Edwardian townhouse that he and Angela had bought a few years earlier.

As he let himself in through the wooden front door with the stained glass inset he heard a screech – "Daaaadddy!" – and like a whirling dervish Little Tom ran down the hall and jumped into his arms. They hugged and rubbed noses vigorously. At the same moment Angela came into the hall to join them and she gave Thom a full blooded kiss. He was taken aback and slow to reciprocate which perturbed him but she did not seem to notice.

"Welcome back. We have missed you, haven't we Little Tom?"

Later he was unsure how he managed to get through the rest of the evening without showing that he was preoccupied and mentally distracted. When they were finally in bed Angela reached under the bedclothes for him but he was unresponsive. He could not explain that his wife's intimacy made him feel unfaithful. Just before he turned over to switch off the light he snuggled up and gave her a more substantial kiss, promising to be more attentive tomorrow. However, as he turned off the light he also apologised for the fact that he would have to attend a

Fellows' Dinner the following evening, a fiction. His dreams that night were disconnected and vivid.

Walking to work the next morning he bought every newspaper he could lay his hands on and scoured them for further details. There was little more revealed about the murder other than an announcement notifying the date and place of the funeral.

At work he was distracted and his colleagues welcomed him back but thought him 'off colour'. During the morning he called Geoffrey Lucas, an old friend and leading member of the Faculty of Chemistry. Thom said that he wanted to 'catch up' and they agreed to meet in the Fellows' Dining Room at seven-thirty.

By early afternoon he could concentrate no longer and so left the office to clear his head. He walked along the 'Backs' hoping the exercise would calm and compose him, but to little avail. At last to fill some time before his meeting with Geoffrey he went and sat in the College chapel. He was aware that there was no logic to this decision but the serenity of the building was tangible.

'Founded in 1441 by King Henry VI the chapel history of King's College has been closely woven into that of the University and Cambridge itself. The choir, made up of sixteen boys between the ages of seven and thirteen, and fourteen undergraduates, sings services six out of every seven days of the week.'

At the moment that Thom entered, however, the building was empty and an almost audible hush surrounded him. He wrapped his coat around himself more tightly.

As he sat deep in thought in one of the seats reserved for senior clergy the young choristers from the College school came bounding in with all the rowdiness and ingenuous pleasure associated with being young and innocent. Gradually the older and more serious choristers arrived and when the Assistant Director of Music took his place they all settled down to concentrate and prepare for evensong.

The main piece for the evening was to be Allegri's *'Miserere'. How very apposite*, he thought.

"It is impossible to hear music in King's and for one's soul to remain troubled," an old friend had said to him once. And as the treble voice reached and sustained the top C the boy's voice hung in the air as if swirling around his head. He wanted to cry at the pure, unadulterated perfection of the sound that so transfixed him. Gradually the maelstrom that had been consuming him began to subside.

As the chapel started to fill for the evening service he slipped out of a side door.

At seven fifteen Thom ordered a whisky & soda in the Fellows' bar and a Gin & French for Geoffrey.

Chuckling, Geoffrey told him that he had been categorised that afternoon by his tailor, when measuring him for a jacket, as 'portly short'. A jolly, rubicund man, he did not immediately command the attention that might be associated with an internationally renowned scientist. He tended not to sit still and was constantly fidgeting with his beloved pipe, forever reaming, cleaning, filling, tamping the tobacco and biting the stem, but only very rarely being able to experience the satisfying pleasure of drawing the smoke deep into his lungs.

Dinner was the usual perfectly prepared meal contrasting the delicacy of 'king prawns and melon with parma ham' for the first course with the strength of 'seared fillet of beef in beetroot jus' for the main. A light 'peppermint sorbet' rounded off the meal before 'cheese and biscuits' arrived with the port. A small, scaled, solid-silver 'train' with three bottles of port rumbled continuously around the long table as it was passed to the left.

After the meal and as they relaxed companionably over coffee in the comfortable leather armchairs of the Senior Common Room, Thom asked Geoffrey nonchalantly if he knew anything about a drug called Myalycin.

Geoffrey considered for a few moments and then, speaking in his usual short-breathed almost staccato fashion, answered:

"Hmm. Pharmacology is not really my bag but it's interesting you should ask. As it happens there have been a few whispers circulating in journals. Some people have begun to ask questions about that little number.

"It has been around for twenty-plus years I should think. When it first came to market it was referred to as a 'wonder drug' and it has made an enormous fortune for the man who first formulated it, one Aristotle Minas.

"There is a rumour that a new version is to be released and that it promises to offer twice the efficacy of the original. Both the FDA, the American regulator, and the UK regulating body are apparently scrutinising it for evidence that it is 'harmful to humans', but so far I haven't heard of any debilitating side effects. It's been around in its original form for a long time now."

"You sound a little sceptical, Geoffrey," said Thom.

"Hmm. Well, as I say, it's not really my area and I have nothing tangible upon which to base any observation other than it's always seemed to me that if something appears too good to be true, then it probably is."

"Not a very empirical observation, or one that stands up to challenge," observed Thom.

"I agree, hence my reluctance to form a judgement, but when whispers start it is often worth looking a little more deeply."

The evening had been genial although Thom did not return home any more at ease.

The Large Hadron Collider at CERN was a project with which Thom had been involved for ten years. As an expert in string theory he had worked almost exclusively developing the theoretical framework that described the point-like particles of particle physics replaced by one-dimensional objects called strings. His project looked to describe how strings propagate through space and interact.

When asked by the scientific world to explain his work he used the string metaphor to explain that, "on distance scales, larger than string scale, a string looks just like an ordinary particle with its mass charge and other properties determined by the vibrational state of the string". At this stage most listeners were confused, but if they were comprehending he would continue.

"In string theory one of the many vibrational states of the string corresponds to the gravitation. A quantum mechanical particle carries gravitational force and thus string theory is a theory of quantum gravity. All of this is theoretical work, but the importance of what we do is to model, superconductors and super insulators. The competition to develop superconductors is fierce. A fortune is to be made when we get there and at CERN we experiment with string theory using the mighty Hadron Collider."

It was the morning of Petra's funeral. Thom had travelled a considerable distance to the crematorium unbidden. He skirted the main throng of mourners in the hope that he might manage a few words with Ariadne, however he accepted that this was probably not going to be possible.

The cortege drew up almost silently and Ariadne descended from the first limousine. As elegant as ever the pain of her suffering only enhanced her beauty, her pale face in stark contrast to the darkness of her hair. Thom was unprepared for the physical impact he experienced at seeing her again.

From behind her in the car emerged a much older man, broad and tall, upright and well-built with a thick moustache and grey flecked wiry hair, her father thought Thom, *Not unlike one of those statues of Stalin.* The man took her right arm and supported her on the short walk into the chapel.

Behind them followed a shorter, slighter man whose drawn features gave a sharp outline to his face highlighting his jaw and high cheekbones. Even from a distance Thom could see that his eyes were compelling, mesmeric but reptilian he thought. It was impossible to make any judgement as to his character, but the personality Thom perceived made him feel uneasy. The man's movements were deliberate, as if calculated, each adjustment of his body reminded Thom of the automata so beloved of AI films. It would be wrong to say that there was a femininity to his mien but an inner strength and steel were discernible; more Thom suspected of the calculating female stiletto type than that of brutal male violence. There was no doubt that he was well toned and probably fit. His oiled and slicked back dark hair hung to his shoulders and it suited his olive skin as did the thin, Errol Flynn moustache that somehow seemed right; definitely attractive to women. Whoever he was he seemed to possess an inner, restrained power and Thom wondered what would be the result if he were crossed. This man emanated control and power.

The younger man was making every effort to be solicitous for Ariadne's well-being but without any apparent affection. *I wonder if that's Dino?* thought

Thom and, irrationally, he felt a wave of anger swoop over him. Both father and husband, if indeed they were, were dressed in dark suits and wore long black cashmere overcoats. They dressed expensively and impeccably.

The coffin followed the mourners into the chapel for the service carried by six young men, probably friends of Petra, but Thom remained outside, his breath a small mist in front of his face. He positioned himself carefully so that she would see him as she returned to the car. She had been wearing large framed dark glasses behind which were hidden both her eyes and her emotions.

Thom stamped and shuffled to ward off the cold and after nearly forty minutes the service concluded. As she arrived back at the car he looked directly into Ariadne's eyes, he knew she must have seen him but she gave no indication of recognition.

As her car drew away Thom found time to think of Petra. He had known her for a number of years before his move to Cambridge as both friend and colleague. She had always been vivacious with an infectious sense of humour and piercingly bright green, pixie eyes, always full of life and fun. A deeper cloud of sadness descended upon him and his mood became ever more sombre. The leaves that had created such a picturesque collage at Ashridge were now sodden and turning to mush on the road.

As he returned to his car for the journey home he was emotional and not least a little bitter at Ariadne's apparent rejection. Had he ever really existed for her, perhaps only as a distraction? Their time, albeit brief, had seemed so much more. Possibly he was just being naïve, but he did not want to accept this conclusion. He knew he had to put all these thoughts to rest and refocus on what mattered: his family – his wife, child and career. Any other possibility had been a romantic fantasy; a spell she had woven around him. At that thought he gave a small wry smile.

Driving back along the M4 and on an impulse he turned off onto the A33 into Reading and sought out the School of Medical Sciences at the University. Doctor Richard Leakey, who headed up the pharmacology and toxicology department, was an acquaintance. By a fortunate coincidence Richard was working in his office that afternoon and was delighted to welcome Thom.

Richard offered Thom a cup of tea and after the courteous preliminaries enquiring after each other's family were out of the way, Richard said, "Something tells me this isn't just a social call, why are you here Thom?"

"You're right. The fact is, and I shall not go into the detail, but I am interested in what you can tell me about a drug called Myalycin."

"Live forever, eh Thom," Richard chuckled. "Give time a run for its money."

"That reminds me of a line of poetry quoted to me by a friend."

"Andrew Marvell. Not all scientists are Philistines

like you, Thom. But to get back to your question, you have identified an interesting product. Myalycin came to the market twenty-six years ago.

"Despite what some people still think drugs used in medicine do not work by magic. They bind to receptors that control the ways the body normally functions and they nudge the control system in the desired direction. To do this, drugs must reach their target receptors and so the absorption, metabolism and excretion of drugs are all important. The adverse effects that drugs and other substances sometimes produce is called toxicology and so before any new drug is licensed for human use the level of toxicology has to be assessed.

"When Myalycin first appeared the pharmaceutical industry did everything in their mighty power to see it refused a licence. None of them could understand why it worked and in the early days they were unable to synthesise a generic equivalent. It must be toxic they all clamoured, but they could not identify any deleterious effect. As the patent period reached expiry there was a frenzy of R & D and at last one of the big boys came up with an alternative, but it never really worked as well.

"You have to understand Thom, the formula for this 'elixir of life' is probably one of the most valuable pieces of chemistry ever undertaken. The opportunity to extend life expectancy by even a small amount is a universal desire."

"Thank you Richard, that is fascinating, but is there anything else you can tell me, perhaps about recent developments?"

"Yes Thom, it's not quite the end of the story. A few months ago Minas Industries sent for testing a new version of Myalycin that it claims can postpone the normal ageing process by more than ten to fifteen years. It won't stave off disease but every organ in the body begins to age from adulthood, imagine if that process can be slowed dramatically. The longer you take the drug the greater the cumulative effect, so it is systemic. Start popping aged twenty-five and the chances of getting to ninety-five, as fit and active as a person of sixty, are greatly enhanced.

"So when some months ago Minas submitted Myalycin 2 for testing we were among those asked to take a look and thus far we have been unable to establish any detrimental effect in the animal tests. Of course we don't know about humans yet, but I think they are encountering a problem about which they are keeping very quiet."

"Good heavens," Thom found himself saying aloud, "Myalycin is a licence to print money almost beyond the dreams of Croesus."

"Yes Thom. But between you and me there is something wrong. I can't prove anything but I think that the way in which some of the chemicals bind to the proteins in the human body is not necessarily the same for all primates, although Minas's results are predicated upon them doing so. They are not being open and truthful because if they were they would have won a Nobel prize by now. In all tests Myalycin proves harmless but if it is benign then what are Minas Industries hiding?

"Apologies, Thom, I have a tutee booked. Great as it is to see you I have to go. I am intensely curious to know though why you sought me out to ask about Myalycin, not an obvious area of interest for a Cambridge physicist."

"I promise to buy you dinner soon and all will be revealed," said Thom as he collected his coat from the back of the door and wished Richard goodbye.

As he walked out of the building his mind was in a whirl trying to make sense of all he had learned, none of which seemed to relate to him in any way other than the name Minas belonged to Ariadne. From the M4 he drove sedately around the M25 and up the M11 back to Cambridge to spend the evening with Angela and Little Tom.

As he turned off the M11 onto the A603 into Cambridge he decided that as he would pass the office he would pop in and pick up his post. It was past six o'clock and most of the department had left for home. There did not seem to be anything of interest or importance in his post box except for an envelope addressed to him in an elegant feminine hand and marked personal. It was postmarked the previous day.

Centuries to grow, how does an ancient tree feel
when the final blow of the axe parts it from its roots?

When I told him
I cried

Something broke
Inside

The door to the fourth dimension
Closed

Our love was forever I
Supposed

But the glass cage in which my love was
forged

Shattered - a small shard cut a brilliant
cord

And, drowning, you slipped from my grip
deep

A mortal wound and still I
Weep

Thom took a few days' leave and when he returned to work he buried himself intensively in the projects for which he was responsible. Each evening he made time to get home reasonably early so that he and Little Tom could be together before bed time and after supper he listened intently to Angela's concerns over the restructuring of the maths department at her school. Regularly he found himself depressed at the state of education in England. He could never understand why rational debate about the purpose of education is not undertaken. All the constant change appeared to him to be driven by ideology and therefore doomed schools to constant change with every new iteration of government. Radical reform of the education system was the only answer; education should be too important to remain in the domain of politicians he concluded.

Term ended and the College was winding down although Thom had one commitment remaining, a convention in Edinburgh to where he had travelled prior to joining the family at Angela's parents for Christmas.

It was three days before Christmas and Little Tom awoke with mounting excitement; he leapt out of bed and ran to his parents' room, his animation bubbling over. Angela was not yet awake, but it was not long before Little Tom had bullied her out of bed and she was packing. Christmas was so close that Little Tom could feel its imminence.

Term had finished for Angela a few days earlier and she and Little Tom were travelling to her parents who lived just outside Hexham in Northumberland. Thom would join the family on the twenty-third.

Managing Little Tom and packing the old Volvo V7 singlehanded was complicated because of the contagion of excitement that Little Tom was spreading through the house, but by mid-morning they had departed and were turning onto the A14 to drive west before heading due north on the A1. Angela felt happy and was looking forward to a quiet Christmas. It was guaranteed that her parents would have everything organised and she would be able to rest for a few days. Some walks in the hills behind the farm with the family would be just the tonic they all needed.

An hour after they had left Pemberton Terrace an inconspicuous light grey, Citroen Berlingo van drew up outside and two men dressed in white overalls, with masks obscuring their features, and elastic gloves on their hands, slid open the side door of the van and retrieved a toolbox. One proceeded to turn off the mains gas inlet to number eleven, while the other gained illegal access in seconds through the front door.

On entering the house, the men undertook a systematic search of the study desk. In no time they found what they were looking for, a small blue notebook containing all the family passcodes for various internet sites and the wireless devices in the house. All of Thom and Angela's passwords were noted in the book, but the men were only interested in those for the router from where they could establish the various IP addresses.

It took time, but they did not hurry. The men worked in silence, adapting the gas pipe where it exited the meter in the house and inserting a two-way switch. When triggered wirelessly the switch would release gas into the house. Satisfied that their handiwork was hardly noticeable and untraceable the men turned their attention to the electrical switch box. They identified the trip that related to the upstairs lighting circuit and swapped it for one they had brought with them. This was also linked to the house wireless network and both devices were now accessible remotely.

The men took enormous care to ensure there was no evidence of their intrusion and when satisfied that their entry and adaptions would not be easily discerned they let themselves quietly out of the front door. The gas main in the road was switched back on. The house was now a potential bomb. At any time of their choosing, probably at night, the valve by the meter could be switched, via the house network, which would then allow the house to fill with gas. The trip mechanism in the electrical cabinet would be set wirelessly and simultaneously so as to arc when a bedside light was turned on. The only unknowns were when the bomb would be detonated and how many adjacent houses would be destroyed in the explosion. The two men replaced the toolbox in the van and drove away sedately.

Christmas passed happily and nine months more ticked by during which time Thom began to regain the equilibrium he had lost. He established a pattern and rhythm to his week and he was settled. The turbulence that had accompanied the end of the previous year diminished and he forced himself not to resurrect memories that contained jagged edges.

A two-week holiday in Rock in Cornwall during August had been very happy with endless walks along the dunes and swims in the sea. They had decided to extend the family when they saw an advert for Labrador pups available from a local kennel. Rufus accompanied them home and turned the house upside down. He was a handful but a much loved addition.

It was almost a year after he had first met Ariadne, and many months since he had seen her last, and just as the academic year was beginning, that the 'bomb' arrived in the form of a letter.

Minas Industries

Athens

Greece

1ˢᵗ September

Dear Professor Miller

I am sure you are aware of the leading position Minas Industries occupies in the world of pharmacology and toxicology. What is less well known is the work undertaken by Minas in the field of physics.

Minas Industries has embarked upon the construction of a small particle accelerator, your area of expertise. Your reputation is such that we would like to consult with you and seek your advice, for which we are prepared to pay a six figure sum, to be agreed.

I write to ask if, initially, you will visit our offices in Athens for a preliminary discussion. If this is acceptable to you then please inform my office when you will be available and arrangements will be made. I assume that it goes without saying that all communication between ourselves must remain confidential.

I look forward to welcoming you to Athens.

Yours sincerely

Dino Minas

Managing Director

PART FOUR

Ariadne

Ariadne lived the days following Petra's death in a surreal oblivion. Her conscious thought was subsumed into a vortex of pain and loneliness and despair. She was hardly aware of the time she spent at the police station where she proved incapable of offering a coherent account of events. The evidence did not implicate her and the constabulary treated her gently, especially once they realised who was her father. Aristotle Minas was alerted to his daughter's plight and the machinery that was the mighty Minas empire was very swift in coming to her assistance.

Within an hour of Aristotle being informed, a top criminal barrister had been engaged from Chambers at 2 Bedford Row and Ariadne was released from custody. A close friend, Evelyn, came to collect her and accompanied her back to a suite at *The Savoy*, where, by the time she arrived, all her belongings from Park Street had been transferred and were neatly arranged in the hope that she would feel comfortable with some familiar surroundings. However, Ariadne seemed not to notice and asked to be left alone. A doctor came to examine her and established the only trauma from which she was suffering was emotional. It would take time and patience before her recovery began. In the meantime, he prescribed a sedative and 30mg of Temazepam to be taken at night.

The emptiness of her mind and the listlessness of her body was gradually replaced by confusion and inertia. Some while later a lucidity descended that enabled her to begin to order events and start to make sense of what had happened, but this was not for a few days.

Her father suspended all his involvement in Minas Industries temporarily and flew to London in the company's private jet landing at City Airport the morning after Petra's death. When he arrived at *The Savoy* he was shown to her room where he was shocked by her mental dislocation, but very moved when she curled up against him on the sofa and hugged him so tightly it was as if she were drawing upon his strength.

Aristotle had the difficult and painful task of meeting Petra's parents when they arrived in London and he accompanied them to the funeral directors where they saw their daughter for the last time. He made the arrangements for the funeral, but it was impossible to set a date because the coroner would not release the body until after the post-mortem.

Aristotle explained to Ariadne that Dino had wanted to accompany him but the doctors at his clinic had advised against him leaving rehabilitation therapy at a critical time. Dino called Ariadne and they talked, but she felt indifferent towards him and when the call was over she wished he hadn't.

Aristotle met with Chief Superintendent Walker to be briefed on what the police had established. Their inclination was to explain events as a robbery that had gone tragically wrong, however there were worrying inconsistencies in this theory. The police had been unable to establish any identity of the killer. A DNA test suggested a man of Mediterranean extraction, but the test could not identify a specific nationality. Where the perpetrator had stayed in London was still a complete mystery. The knife that had killed Petra was specialised and could only be purchased illegally in the UK. Forged from a combination of lightweight metals, it was known to be preferred by covert agents and assassins.

From the forensics examination of the flat it was concluded the man had entered through the front door having bypassed all the security systems. A very sophisticated burglar. Having gained entry, he had searched the bedrooms thoroughly before exiting through the window, probably when he heard Petra return, but then he had waited on the fire escape for Ariadne. Why had he not made his escape over the roofs then?

The man's clothing was lightweight combat gear, the sort preferred by special forces when in the field. A fingerprint trawl through Interpol records had not turned up an identity. There were imponderable questions. Was this a botched kidnap? Was there something of special significance that Ariadne knew? Were there valuables in the flat for which he needed access codes? Was he intending to kill her or did he only intend to intimidate her? The theory of a failed robbery seemed the most likely and was the preferred line of inquiry, but it was a line of inquiry that was leading nowhere.

For Ariadne the days leading up to Christmas passed in dull succession. Aristotle wanted her to return to Athens with him, but she was adamant that she was staying until after the funeral. Aristotle had new carpets laid in the Mayfair flat and instructed an estate agent to put it up for sale. She did not want to stay at *The Savoy* and so father and daughter looked for a new home. In the end she decided to rent a mews flat off Upper Wimpole Street. Aristotle had a security company install the best and most sophisticated system available, which included surveillance and a panic room. When Ariadne was safely established he returned to Athens promising to return for the funeral which was now arranged for the sixth of January.

Ariadne's recovery was slow but gradually each day she managed more easily and by Christmas Eve she felt the need to get out of the flat, stretch her legs and walk. She set off without any particular route in mind. From Harley Street she wandered around Cavendish Square Gardens and then on into Regent Street. The Christmas lights reminded her that the season of comfort and joy was upon the world and she enjoyed the effort made by all the big department stores to engage the attention of shoppers. Without noticing the passing of time she found herself at Piccadilly Circus. Where next? It occurred to her that there was little food in the house and so she decided to wend her way back to the flat via Fortnum & Mason.

As she was walking along Piccadilly she became aware of the sound of a church bell and to her surprise she recognised that she was passing the

Church of St James on her left where she and Thom
had listened to the *Messiah*. There was a board fixed to
the railings announcing a performance of J S Bach's
Mass in B minor, and when she glanced at her watch
she realised that it was about to begin. Without
making a conscious decision she entered the church
and took the stairs to the gallery. She chose to sit
where she and Thom had been perched on the
evening of the *Messiah,* in thrall to the music and each
other. This time, daylight flooded through the large
windows and on either side of the altar was a
Christmas tree, each with colourful lights proclaiming
goodwill. The feel of the place was different, but the
music and voices began to merge and once again
affected her mood; for the first time in days she
began to feel at peace, her disposition matched by
that of the Latin Mass. As the *Sanctus* soared around
her she felt comforted and protected for the first time
since the awful events in which she still felt trapped.
When the final exultant *Gloria* rang out she reached
for Thom's hand, but of course he was not there.

Ariadne had sat and listened to the Mass for nearly
two hours. Gradually day had turned to night and the
church lighting had illuminated the orchestra and
choir, imbuing them with a radiance, or so it seemed
to her overheated mind. The undercurrents of her
troubled spirit tossed her thoughts in different
directions, but they always returned to Petra. The
times they had spent together, their lives woven from
different threads but inextricably linked; their hopes,
desires and sadnesses experienced through the same
lens. Petra's absence was an abyss into which Ariadne
looked and all she felt was despair. The fact that
Petra's death was a sacrifice that had saved Ariadne's

life only compounded the sense of desolation she was feeling. And, as her mind recycled her unhappiness she was transported back to the same space in which she sat now, but some weeks earlier. Then, in a moment of epiphany, she realised the truth that she had been avoiding. She was experiencing two deaths. Thom had not been a distraction, he had entered her soul and she knew that she would never love again with the same absorption, passion or abandonment. Her present mood was without doubt a hopelessness deriving from her loss of one and rejection of the other, the absence of the two people who were her emotional counterpoint, her twin towers.

She walked rapidly back to the flat, found her journal and began to write. The words flowed onto the page carving her misery and loss in black ink onto a page of startlingly white paper[7].

Christmas and the days following were spent quietly. Since her revelation at St James' she was more calm. The acceptance of the fact that she had won and lost Thom enabled her to establish a precarious inner serenity that had been absent since Oxford. It was a productive literary period and she wrote a number of poems through which she hoped to analyse her feelings for Thom. One of these she placed in an envelope that she addressed to his office

---

[7] Refer *Lifelonging* Part 14

in College.

She received a letter from Dumbledore who informed her that her dissertation was being considered for a Distinction. He invited her to attend the following week for a 'viva voce', after which she would be informed of the final result. The poems she had been writing she collected together in a file which she labelled with the working title *'Lifelonging'*.

Her father was due to fly back into London on the day before the funeral and she was expecting him in the late afternoon. It was reassuring that he would be with her during the ordeal. However, she was completely unprepared for the shock of his arrival accompanied by Dino.

Dino was felicitous for her well-being and exuded sympathy for all she had undergone. His handsome features were better ordered than she had expected given the period of time he had been in rehab, and in fact she could detect no physical evidence that he had been unwell. Meeting her husband, she had expected to feel gratitude, affection and relief from which she would draw strength, but the reality was that she found his presence faintly distasteful and there was a gulf, a cold remoteness between them.

To her great relief her father said he and Dino were booked to stay at *The Savoy*. The awkwardness between husband and wife continued that evening and finally it was agreed they would all meet early the next morning and travel together to Petra's parents in Hampshire. The cremation was to take place near Petra's parents' home. As father and son-in-law were preparing to leave Dino picked up the letter addressed to Thom, which she had placed on a table near the door, and offered to post it for her. She could think of no reason to refuse his generosity.

She resolved to get through the funeral by putting her mind into neutral and emptying it of thought. The service was worse than she could have imagined and when afterwards she saw Thom she wanted to run into his arms. However, with an enormous effort of will she managed to remain impassive, despite the fact that she knew he was there for her. She stumbled and Dino took her arm and helped her into the car.

That evening her father discussed her immediate future and what was to happen next. He wanted her to return to Athens. She could live with him until Dino was fully recovered, and then they could move back together. Aristotle wanted her to join Minas Industries and prepare for a senior Board position in due course. She said that she had thought of remaining in England to undertake a PhD, but both men were adamant that they wanted her to return to Athens and she lacked the energy to oppose them. Deep down she knew that she had come to the end of her time in England and her years as a student were over.

Her return to Oxford two days later was unsettling and while the 'Viva' seemed to go well with an animated discussion about the radical shift in English literature between 1890 and 1930, she left College drained and wanting to escape. Her Distinction was confirmed.

The day before she left London she knew that something remained to be sorted out in her mind. She walked, briskly this time, back to St James' Church. As she entered there was a woman creating a flower arrangement, she was giving quiet instruction. "Cut the stems at forty-five degrees as this allows the greatest surface area so that the most water can be absorbed. Use a knife not scissors as scissors will crush the stems and damage them."

Ariadne walked along the nave until she reached the front row of the pews where she sat facing the altar. Time seemed to slow as the peace of the building began to silt into her consciousness, but then her reverie was interrupted by a voice, a man who was obviously speaking to her. He spoke with a gentle tone and an Irish lilt.

"How do you hold a moonbeam in your hand?" he said.

"I'm sorry," said Ariadne, "I don't understand."

"I've brought you a cup of tea and a rich tea biscuit. You looked so sad sitting there and there's nothing like a cup of tea and a rich tea biscuit when you can't quite work things out. May I join you for a moment?"

"Of course." She watched the cleric as he walked around the front of the pew, genuflecting as he passed in front of the altar. *What a lovely little act of love,* she thought.

"Let me explain," said the cleric. "Last night I watched *The Sound of Music*, again, with my children. It is their absolutely favourite film and I like it because it is all about innocence, growing up and the important things in our lives – 'brown paper parcels tied up with string' – all the excitement, pleasure and hope of Christmas in the every day. One song asks, 'How do you hold a moonbeam in your hand?'"

As he said this he retrieved from his cassock a child's bubble blower and pulled the trigger, the air was suddenly filled with glistening suds that glimmered and floated around their heads.

"Watch," he said and as the light reflected off each bubble it changed shape before disappearing suddenly in a tiny explosion.

"I'm sorry," said Ariadne, "I still don't follow."

"Well, all that wonder in the film is threatened when a curtain is drawn back to reveal the brutal beast that has been slouching in the background. You look to me as if you have glimpsed behind the curtain and what you have seen has taken away your hope and peace. Your bubbles have deserted you, your moonbeam has been lost.

"But, consider where you are sitting now, albeit briefly, and remember those wonderful lines of John Betjeman that I can never get out of my head:

And is it true
This most tremendous tale of all,
Seen in a stained-glass window's hue,

A baby in an ox's stall?
The Maker of the stars and sea
Became a Child on earth for me?[8]

"The maker of the stars and sea. Can you see beyond the stars?" Ariadne asked.

He thought for a moment and then replied, "The cloths of heaven disguise what is behind the stars, but the meaning is glimpsed all the time in the bubbles. The flowers, the music, the parcel tied up with string and the peace of this place may only exist for a moment but they remain with you and in each is a tiny glimpse of what's beyond the stars.

"For whatever it is that you grieve, it was part of God's moonbeam. You have held in your hand God's moonbeam, however fleetingly, because the maker of the moon and stars became a child on earth for you and me. The moon may have gone behind a cloud, but it will shine again and in the meantime you have your memories, your bubbles. Now, I must go. God bless you."

"Goodbye," she said, "and thank you for the tea."

Ariadne boarded the Emirates flight EKS 102 from Heathrow Terminal 3 to Athens at 13.20 exactly

---

[8] *'Christmas'* – see Part 15

one week after the funeral. Her father had insisted she travel first class for the three hour thirty-five minute flight. When the plane landed en route to Dubai she was met and ushered swiftly through the Greek border control and then whisked through the crowded city to her father's home in the Plaka region of the city. 'Plaka is recognised as the most picturesque quarter at the heart of Athens with its paved streets and neoclassical houses, a wealthy and relaxing neighbourhood'. As agreed in London Ariadne returned to her father's home and Dino did not raise any objection.

Coming home was the tonic she needed and for some time she did little other than relax in her natural environment. She walked endlessly, almost compulsively, as though she could walk off her black moods. She revisited old haunts in Athens and discovered numerous places previously unknown. The return to her home country felt natural and she revived her interest in the richness of Ancient Greece. Achilles, Odysseus, Hector, Agamemnon – she learned of their deeds and misdeeds – as well as the acts of the gods, bloody to say the least. The wanderings of Theseus and the suffering of poor Helen, the daughter of Leda, raped by Zeus disguised as a swan[9]. She was drawn back to thoughts of Oxford and her love of the poetry of W B Yeats. Then there were the Eumenides, the Furies, who circle the earth seeking out those humans impudent enough to offend the gods and who are then pursued relentlessly until sins are atoned. Was she one of their victims? However, the more she sought escape from

---

[9] 'Leda and the Swan' – see Part 15

her sadness through activity and inertia, the more she found that memories of Thom proved obdurately repetitive. In fact, the intensity of her memories only seemed to deepen.

Ariadne went to visit her mother in the vain hope that the woman she had adored would be lucid enough to discuss the confusions that plagued her, but she was met with a blank wall of indifference. Her mother had passed into another realm from which she would not return. Another loss.

Ariadne's marriage to Dino remained in an enigmatic state. He seemed to show little interest in her and she had not been invited back to what had been her home. She remained living at Plaka with her father and the two established an easy, companionable routine that suited them both.

In the first week of March she started as a senior management trainee with Minas Industries. She would spend some time working in each department before, ultimately, becoming a full Board member. Despite her lack of experience, she learned quickly and possessed an acute understanding of corporate principles; there seemed little doubt that she would make a valuable addition to the empire. When she started she had no knowledge or understanding of the pharmaceutical industry, but within a short while she developed a comprehensive product knowledge and an incisive understanding of Minas Industries products.

Ariadne applied herself with total focus and was soon accorded the respect she deserved within the organisation. Her personal life was secondary to work and her whole purpose for being became Minas Industries.

One day in late October, and much to her surprise, she received a memo from the Managing Director, her husband, asking her to attend a meeting at eleven o'clock, the following day, Thursday morning.

What might Dino want? Presumably it was a business matter, but when she stopped and thought about why she had been summoned, matters were not clear in her mind. Why had Dino remained so distant? She had not wanted to disturb the status quo and so when they were together she avoided any conversation that might provoke a discussion about the future. She recognised that all the passion she had once held for him had vanished; she was now independent and self-sufficient and comfortably so. *I wonder if he wants to talk about my future involvement in the company?* she pondered.

Ariadne always dressed demurely, but with style. Her business suits were hand-made and set off by pure silk shirts under which she often wore a chemise that emphasised her breasts, but discreetly so. By both highlighting and covering her figure she managed to give off enough of a suggestion of femininity to leave the men with whom she worked aware of her presence, but not dominated by her sexuality. If she wore trousers they were cut to hug her waist and if she chose a skirt the length would be just above the knee, usually with dark Wolford sheer tights that showed off her shapely legs to great effect. Her shoes were all made by Gucci in Florence, practical, smart and comfortable. On the morning of her meeting with Dino she spent more time than usual on her makeup and she chose a trouser suit, one of her favourites, that was particularly close fitting.

She did not want to excite his masculinity, but she did want him to be aware of her power as a woman. She added a Liberty scarf clasped by a small diamond broach her father had given her for her last birthday. She carried a small executive leather case containing her laptop, notepad and Mont Blanc fountain pen.

At one minute to eleven Dino's secretary ushered her into his office, a large comfortable space with two panoramic windows, one looking out towards the Parthenon and the other over the new Science and Technology Park that was expanding rapidly – "the new and old worlds that constitute the greatness of modern Greece," as Dino explained.

He was solicitous in every respect and asked numerous questions about her role and involvement in the company, and he went to considerable lengths to emphasise how much her contribution was valued. After a while he brought the conversation round to the topic she could tell he wanted to discuss.

"I want to take this opportunity to talk about us and to ask you a favour. As for us I need to explain why I may have appeared remote, not exactly the loving husband you might have expected since your return. The truth of the matter is that I have met someone else.

"While in the clinic I grew fond of Demetrius and we have become very close since then. However, as you know the most important element of my life is Minas Industries and my loyalty is to the company above all else. The truth of the matter is that we – your father, me and you – need an heir. It was established when we married that there is no blood relation between us and so there can be no objection to my fathering your child. I believe the time has come. You may retain the freedom to live your own life, as long as nothing you do threatens the company, and I shall maintain my relationship with Demetrius.

"But, and I know that this all sounds coldly transactional, especially if we talk about artificial insemination, it is perfectly possible for us to live independently in the same house and for the world to see us as Mr and Mrs Minas."

Ariadne was stunned, but before she had the opportunity to marshal her thoughts Dino continued.

"As for the favour. We have a very important visitor this weekend who I hope will be joining MI soon. I would like you to look after him over the few days of his visit and show him Athens."

She found herself saying that of course she would be pleased to help. "What is his name?"

"Professor Thomas Miller."

PART FIVE

Thom

It had taken Thom longer than he ever imagined it would to impose discipline on his emotions and to force all thoughts of Ariadne into a compartment of his mind where he would visit only on request. Almost nine months had passed since he had last seen her at the funeral and it was only recently that he realised he could get through successive days without her image floating unbidden into his thoughts.

Each year Thom spent the month of September, prior to the start of term, living in Geneva and working at CERN where he and his small team were allowed access to the Super Proton Synchrotron (SPS) to pursue their particular area of research. The SPS was first opened in 1976, but over the years the laboratory had built new accelerators and the original had undergone numerous modifications; the intensity of its proton beam had increased a thousand fold. It was a better choice for their research than the mighty Hadron Collider.

Under Thom's leadership, the King's team hypothesised that some chemical reactions, undertaken by exposing particular elements to the vibrations created in the SPS, changed their properties so dramatically that new chemicals could be formed. The chemical bonding that resulted from the process was unique and the changed valences of these chemicals could be designed to create new versions of existing drugs. An exciting departure from conventional thinking about string theory and superconductors.

Thom had replied promptly to Dino Minas accepting, in principle, his invitation to visit Athens and had said that he might be available to visit sometime in the new year.

In the early hours of a morning in the second week of September, in a darkened room far south of England a hand moved a mouse and a monitor flickered into life. Deliberately certain commands were typed and at number 11 Pemberton Terrace two switches were activated.

Angela was embarking upon the new academic year full of enthusiasm for the challenges that came with her promotion to Head of Department. That evening she was tired and knew that she would sleep soundly as an early night was in order. She set the alarm for 6.30am and when it buzzed it was through a haze of early morning muddle that she reached out to switch on the bedside light.

Thom was deep in thought and considering the ramifications of changing the parameters from the previous day's experiment when his mobile phone rang. It was eight o'clock in the morning and he had already showered and shaved, but was not yet dressed. It was a call from England but not a number he recognised. The caller introduced himself as a policeman.

"I am sorry to report Professor that there has been a gas explosion in Pemberton Terrace. It would be best if you returned to Cambridge immediately," the official voice remaining calm.

"Has anyone been hurt?"

"As yet we have not been able to establish any facts, but had anyone been in number eleven it is difficult to believe they could have survived."

"My wife and young son are at home."

"It would be best if you returned to Cambridge as soon as possible, Professor Miller."

The flight from Geneva to Stansted was delayed and it took a number of hours before Thom was back at the site of the devastation, by which time a fire crew had the situation under control. Three bodies had been recovered, a woman and a child from number eleven and a man from number twelve, also the remains of a young dog. All were unrecognisable and would have to be identified from dental records. Thom was asked for the name of the family's dentist.

Friends rallied around. Charlie and Mary insisted that Thom come to stay with them; he was only operating on a basic level and was too numb to make any decisions. They took him under their wing. The College immediately placed him on compassionate leave and the Dean stressed that he was not to have any concerns about university duties for the present.

For the next couple of weeks, he was unable to process thoughts or make decisions, the enormity of the tragedy was too great for him to comprehend. The only positive thoughts that did come to him were happy dreams of playing with Little Tom and being comfortable in Angela's arms, but the waking reality was almost too great to bear. When he considered the unfairness, the obliteration of innocents, the random confluence of devastating circumstance, the only conclusions he could reach confirmed his opinion that there is no point in appealing to, or railing against, some abstract and implacable deity. Moreover, if there were an omniscient being, a God that allowed such a tragedy as this to unfold, then that would be such a crime against humanity that no feeling person would venerate him. At least arbitrary events resulting in a catastrophe are understandable on a logical level.

Two weeks after the dire event Thom received a call from a senior policeman at the Cambridge Constabulary's headquarters at Hinchingbrooke Park, Huntingdon. Gently Detective Inspector Andrew Wilson asked Thom to visit him at his earliest convenience. It concerned a matter of some urgency.

At first Thom thought he would postpone a visit, but then he realised that he had no priority, no one to look after or return home for, and so he found himself driving out to Huntingdon that afternoon.

Andrew Wilson was a tall, lean, grave man, certainly humourless but reassuring in the measured way he spoke and analysed the evidence available to him. After sending for two cups of tea and settling Thom into a chair in his office he began:

"Professor Miller I fear that the news I have to impart will come as a further shock and will be highly distressing for you. Number eleven Pemberton Terrace has now been searched and the site painstakingly examined by our forensic teams. The conclusion we have reached is that your family were murdered. We do not expect you to be able to weigh the implications around such an event in a short space of time, but we are going to have to ask for your help, consideration and assistance to move our investigation forward."

It was as if Thom had not heard what had been said. Andrew Wilson was a patient man and at last Thom asked the inevitable question, "Why?"

"If we knew that, Professor, then we would be halfway to solving a crime, but as it is there seems to be no discernible motive, which is why we need your help."

"What is the evidence that has led you to this conclusion?"

"Well the gas inlet has been tampered with and was opened remotely by means of a wireless connection with your broadband. It was operated by using the house network and a switch that allowed the house to fill with gas overnight. One of the electrical trip switches was also tampered with and set to arc when a light was turned on, probably the bedside lamp. The explosion took place at 6.30am, as far as we can establish."

"Do you suspect me of involvement, Superintendent?"

"We have no evidence to that effect, Professor, and while your involvement is possible our investigation does not immediately include you as a suspect."

"So what happens next?"

"You are a rational man, Professor Miller, and we would like you to apply your mind and consider any motive, however irrational. Given the oxidation on the pipe we think the device has been in place for some months. In which case were you meant to be a victim? From all we know of your wife she led an exemplary life.

"We know that the funeral of your wife and son are to take place next week. We would be grateful if you will come to see us when that is over and together we can rake through any evidence we have collected."

For Thom it was a matter of getting past the funeral. He had found the whole project of organising the event enormously harrowing. Deciding upon hymns and the form of the service was a living nightmare, but it was the least he could do for Angela and their 'Little Angel'. The intensity of the furnace following the explosion was such that the human remains recovered from the fire were light and insubstantial and it was agreed that mother and child could be buried together in one coffin.

Finally, the ordeal was over and Thom was at a loss to know where to start to begin reconstructing his life. If the police were correct in their supposition then there had to be a motive, this being a carefully prepared crime.

He sifted through all he knew about Angela and could think of no reason why she would be the intended victim, and of course it was beyond belief that Little Tom had been the target. Therefore, someone must have wanted him dead, but the 'bomb' had been detonated when he was away from home, was that accident, incompetence or just bad planning? While the work he was involved with was secret and had potential value in the commercial market its secrets certainly did not justify killing a family. He discussed all his thoughts with Andrew Wilson, but nothing made sense. The detective said it had proved impossible to trace the internet connection that initiated the explosion and the investigation was heading up a blind alley. The superintendent had no objection to Thom going overseas on a holiday if he so chose.

"There is of course one other scenario we have not considered," said Andrew at their last meeting. "Revenge?"

For the following weeks Thom was rudderless. He visited Angela's parents and his own and took out a rental on a flat in the centre of Cambridge. He knew that he would be unable to focus at work and so took an indefinite leave of absence, but he became increasingly aware that he could not continue to drift aimlessly. After a while he recalled the invitation to visit Athens and wrote to Dino Minas to say that he would be available for a visit in November. He received a prompt reply confirming that a plane ticket had been reserved. Minas Industries were looking forward to his visit.

In the first week of November, Thom boarded a Ryanair flight from Stansted to Athens and experienced a sense of release as he stepped onto the aircraft to leave England behind. The flight was straightforward and he was met at Athens by a driver who took him to a very comfortable hotel near the centre of Athens. In rather poor English the driver explained that he would return at 9.00am the following morning to take Thom to Minas Industries where he would meet Dr Dino Minas, the Managing Director.

That evening Thom sat outside a small restaurant and there was still enough warmth in the November air for him to feel comfortable. Later he realised that he had managed a couple of hours without being drawn into the well of despair that had incapacitated him since that fateful day.

Having slept relatively restfully he was ready for

collection at the agreed time.

The headquarters of Minas Industries was an impressive building designed by one of Athens' most bold and daring architects. The shape of the place and the materials used to build it gave a sense of lightness, of space and gleaming confidence. No expense had been spared and the design that radiated off a central, vaulted concourse was vaguely reminiscent of a cathedral with transepts, buttresses, cloisters and large colourful windows allowing light to flow through the building. Rather apposite, thought Thom, a new cathedral from where the worship of Mammon in the modern world is practised.

Dino Minas could not have been more charming and welcoming. He was at pains to stress how privileged the company was that Professor Thomas Miller was visiting. He was especially appreciative as he knew of the awful events that had transpired recently in Thom's life.

Turning to the purpose of the meeting he wanted to explain:

"The Minas Industries research and development all takes place on Crete in special laboratories that were created particularly to develop Myalycin. We are now working on a second-generation drug.

"The intersection of our interest and the reason for the invitation is that Minas Industries have built a small particle accelerator. It is a much smaller version than that at CERN, but big enough for us to experiment on chemical structures such as those of interest to you and us.

"My hope is, Professor, that you will visit our

laboratories on Crete and help us to progress our experimentation a stage further. If you agree then I would like you to visit the island for a few months and work with us. I have had a contract drawn up and you will certainly be attracted by the salary, which is generous by any measure. Perhaps being away from England at this time would help you to come to terms with your appalling loss.

"But you are now in Athens for a few days and I have organised for a senior Minas executive to show you our wonderful city."

Saying this, he went to his desk and pressed a button. The door opened and in walked Ariadne.

Had he been conscious of anything he would have been aware of Dino studying him intensely, but he was utterly confused.

"My wife has offered to be your guide. I don't think you have met. Ariadne, this is Professor Thomas Miller.

"Forgive me, Professor," said Dino, "I fear that I have another matter to which I must attend and so I shall leave you both to get to know one another."

Ariadne said, "A pleasure to meet you, Professor. Perhaps I may call at your hotel at seven-thirty this evening and we shall find somewhere to eat? I will be driving. I hope this arrangement meets with your approval?"

"It does," said Thom and at last he dropped her hand. They each went their own way.

It was exactly seven-thirty when Ariadne drew up outside the hotel in her Mercedes 350 Sport Coupe convertible. A casual onlooker might have concluded that she had dressed with studied indifference, but exactly the opposite was the case and a closer inspection would have revealed that she radiated femininity.

Initially they were tongue tied. There was so much to say and Ariadne knew they had to start with the horror. "Thom, I was so sorry to hear of your loss."

"I seem to remember someone saying to me that, 'the ancients were never wrong about suffering,'" replied Thom.

"You are in Greece now," said Ariadne. "We invented suffering. Come along, I know a wonderful taverna that cooks the most delicious lobster, let's go."

She drove with efficiency and speed. The car hugged the contours of the road and it was not long before they had left the city centre behind. She increased speed and when they came up behind a slower vehicle she used the paddles on the steering wheel to drop the gears and overtake with precision. She braked into the bends and accelerated out with adept judgement; he felt secure with her at the wheel. They travelled in virtual silence, each wondering what the other would have to say, both nervous and confused as to how the conversation would progress.

Ariadne drove them to a small restaurant outside the city. It was a dark night and the tables were detached, each set under a small thatched umbrella. She wore a cardigan over the 1950s frock that she had chosen for the evening. It showed off her figure, which had shed a few pounds since her return, and she hoped that he liked what he saw. Dressed in dark chinos with a light blue Ralph Lauren shirt and yellow pullover, she scrutinised him for any sign of remoteness. They were soon seated, and after the waiter had taken their orders they looked each other in the eyes for the first time since they had met that afternoon.

"Will you tell me what happened in Cambridge?" asked Ariadne.

"Well the details are simple, a gas explosion that destroyed my life as I knew it. The police say it was deliberate and are seeking a murderer. For a while I thought they suspected me as the only one with a motive, although rightly, they could not conceive why I would want to blow my family apart, literally.

"Coincidentally, I had received a letter a couple of months ago from Dino inviting me here. Once the awfulness and despair receded slightly and after the funeral, I decided to accept Dino's offer and so here I am. I'm not sure what else I can tell you. What happened to you after Petra's death?"

"I also was a suspect for a while, but in the end the conclusion was that I was the intended victim. The case became cold and is probably on a shelf somewhere. There has been no further attempt on my life and none of what happened makes any sense. I joined MI as a trainee and recently my husband informed me that he is gay and does not want me living with him, although he wants me to father his IVF child to ensure a dynasty. In a nutshell that sums up my life since we parted a year ago."

The lobster was served and was delicious. They ordered a bottle of Sancerre and it complemented the firm texture and subtle flavour of the crustacean. Their conversation was at first desultory and neither seemed ready to raise the subject of their parting in Oxford almost exactly a year before.

"Are you thinking of accepting Dino's offer of work at the laboratories on Crete?" enquired Ariadne.

"I have my work at the College but every street in Cambridge reminds me of Little Tom and Angela. The Dean has told me that I may stay away for as long as I need and so the answer is yes. Having a project a long way from Cambridge appeals."

"As it happens I am being seconded to Crete to complete my management training and so we might meet up, if you would like to that is. I grew up in Crete and so I could show you around."

"I think that would be wonderful."

As he helped her up from the table he took her hand and they walked to the car. Neither was aware of a small white van parked to one side of the car park or of the two men munching sandwiches silently. They drove back to the hotel, again in virtual silence.

Before they parted Thom said, "Dino emailed me this afternoon and asked that I meet him on Sunday morning to give him my decision. My flight back to Stansted leaves early afternoon and so I shall have to get to the airport by midday."

"Well tomorrow is Saturday. Will you let me show you around Athens?"

"That would be lovely."

Thom was staying in the Plaka Hotel on Kaprikareas Street, a short distance from where Ariadne lived, and so she chose to walk over. They met for coffee on the hotel terrace, which has a fine and uninterrupted view across to the Acropolis, dominated by the Parthenon.

"Greece is a city of such contradictions," said Ariadne when the coffee had arrived. "The old gods were a rum lot, very violent and at times bestial. Murder and rape abounded. Chronos, the father of the gods, ate his children because a prophecy had said one of them would kill him. Rhea, his wife, escaped to Crete and secretly gave birth to her sixth child, a son, Zeus, in a cave. Zeus went on to rape Leda and she gave birth to Helen who of course was Helen of Troy and so it goes on.

"But then Athens invents democracy, not exactly as we understand it, but eventually the ideas of those ancient Greeks become the foundations of our political system and the freedoms we fight so hard to protect. The philosophy, mathematics, architecture, poetry, drama that we know all stem from here. It is a city of enormous paradoxes, as I said, and a wonderful place to live."

"Does it take long to walk to the Acropolis?" asked Thom. "I would love to visit."

Ariadne picked up her handbag. "Let's go."

Ariadne was trying to interpret Thom's mood, but it was difficult. Was he being distant because he did not want to be with her? Was he feeling guilt about their relationship and his wife and was he going to dash her hope of a reconciliation, albeit a platonic one?

She heard herself prattling, "The noun Parthenon actually means 'unmarried women's apartments', but nobody is entirely sure what happened there. The Acropolis is dedicated to Athena who is the goddess of knowledge, purity, arts, justice and wisdom. She represents intelligence, humility, creativity, education, enlightenment, truth, justice and moral values. She was a canny and sassy girl."

"A suitable description of someone I know," said Thom ruefully, and she smiled.

Pretending to ignore him she continued, "Her brother, Ares, on the other hand was a nasty piece of work – the patron of violence, bloodlust and slaughter. I said they were a rum bunch."

Ariadne kept up her commentary until they had

entered the Parthenon and until she began to sense that Thom might need a little time on his own, and so she said that she was off to the shop to buy a book and would be back soon. She timed her absence for a quarter of an hour. As she returned she saw Thom sitting on the base of a large broken pillar with his head down as if deep in thought. She walked up to him and put her hand under his chin and tilted his head upwards so that he was looking at her directly. He was crying. Tears were welling up from somewhere deep inside him and running silently down his cheeks to fall into the dusty ground where they were instantly absorbed.

In a moment of total empathy, she sat beside him and wrapped her arms around him, and they remained there, side by side, for a long time.

Later, back at the hotel over an evening coffee, and tucked away in a private corner of the bar, she said, "You wrote me a sonnet."

"It seemed appropriate," he replied.

"What seemed appropriate? Was it the lovely metaphor of planets joined but permanently separated, or was it because a sonnet is a love poem?"

"You asked me once what lies behind the stars and I did not understand the question. When I met you for the first time I was utterly disorientated, but then it was as if a curtain were drawn aside and I was allowed a glimpse of some truth beyond my understanding. I have come to think that it is you who lies beyond the stars, Ariadne.

"You might not want me to say this, but from the moment you first entered my life, nothing else seemed as important as the time I spent with you. It was mesmerising and confusing. And then when you rejected me it was as if the moon and stars fell out of the sky. I have loved you, I think, from the very first minute we met. After you sent me away I tried to be a good husband and father, they loved me dearly, but now they are gone. Did I wish for that? No, of course not."

When she left him later that evening her heart was filled with sadness for the dejected man she left behind, he was still wrapped in a carapace of suffering that she could not penetrate.

The following morning Thom and Dino met. The meeting was succinct and it was agreed that Thom would be engaged to advise Minas Industries and would live on Crete until the expiry of his contract. They parted on amicable terms and Thom could not bring himself to think of Dino as a rival.

Ariadne stood at the plate glass window of the terminal at Athens airport and watched as the Ryanair flight took to the air. She waved but then felt foolish. Her hand rested on the glass as if she were reaching for something and she whispered a few words that nobody heard before she turned and made her way back to the life she had chosen, as if strapped to a wheel of fire.

At the same moment two inconspicuous men left Dino's office and walked back slowly to their small van.

PART SIX

Hani

The journey from the Libyan coastline to Crete had been exhilarating; it was in complete contrast to that of the preceding few weeks. This time the hours seemed to fly, literally, as the boat skimmed across the waves so fast that Hani's hair was blown uncontrollably behind her. She held fast to her hijab and in the end had to settle for tying it around her neck as a scarf, that being the only safe way to preserve it. The dust and sand of the desert was washed from her face as spray flew from the bow of the Zodiac that was whisking them across the sea. The crew were inscrutable and the only information she gleaned was their destination. The name did not mean a great deal to her, but she was very happy that an island belonging to Greece was to be their journey's end.

She had been dreading the crossing to Europe, there were so many tales of journeys that ended tragically. She had seen pictures in magazines of the bodies of refugees, especially children, washed up on a shore, but these sailors had given her a life jacket and a pullover. After all the stories she had heard of danger and exploitation it seemed to her that she had been blessed and she wondered if maybe her father had managed to negotiate this safe passage, if so she would be forever grateful. In her morning prayers she also gave profound thanks to Allah for his intervention on her behalf.

Eventually, exhausted, she found a small space under a bulwark where she could curl up and she slept. There had been no moon but as she awoke with the pre-dawn the stars were beginning to fade and Crete loomed large, dark and silhouetted on the horizon. They were approaching rapidly, but then the engines were throttled back and with the crisp early light of sunrise she could make out that they were heading for a bay dominated by a large white building situated on a hillside some few hundred metres above the shore. There was only the one residence and it seemed enormous compared with any dwelling she had ever seen before; it was painted brilliant white and a single road wound away from the house through a forest of low trees, probably olive groves she thought.

The Zodiac glided the last few metres alongside the jetty before the reverse thrust brought them close enough for two of the crew, fore and aft, to jump ashore and make the boat secure, followed almost immediately by the second vessel carrying the men. As with all their movements the sailors were quick, efficient and uncommunicative. Apart from offering their charges bottled water there had been no dialogue for the length of the passage.

At the end of the jetty a minibus was parked and it was gestured to them that they were to board. When all were seated they were joined by a driver and a woman who was as loquacious as the sailors had been silent. She chatted away to them in a common language telling them about the island. She informed them that Crete grew more olive trees than any other island in the Mediterranean and she explained how the olives were harvested and how the milling process was undertaken within twenty-four hours of picking. She kept talking throughout the drive detailing the flora and fauna. Disconcertingly, she had a habit of instructing the driver to stop and she would leap out, pluck a wild herb and then hand it around instructing them to savour the aroma. She did succeed at putting them at their ease and it was not long before they arrived at the house that she had seen from the bay.

There are over a hundred different languages spoken across Sudan, but the most common is Sudanese Arabic. The woman who had accompanied them in the bus spoke clear Arabic and with a dialect that they could all understand. On arrival they were settled in a large room and she began by welcoming them to Crete.

They were seated in an extensive room in the mansion and their mentor began by explaining that they were extremely fortunate. A Greek millionaire had made it his mission to alleviate the plight of as many refugees as possible by helping them to reach and pass through Greece into northern Europe. They would stay for a few weeks while their refugee status was established and their sanctuary arranged and later they would be helped to pass on to the European country of their choice.

Not one among them was used to European customs or furniture and while they found the room comfortable they did not feel settled. They were disorientated, not only by the furnishings, but also by the speed of events, however all were incredulous at their good fortune.

Their instructor continued. "You must first decide which is to be your chosen country and our benefactor will look to get you placed. You must get used to the way people live in Europe and study their habits, you are to learn the basics of the language of the country in which you want to settle. England is the most difficult to enter so please don't all say you want to go there. Germany is presently the most hospitable."

She continued. "You are welcome here and it will be your home for a while, but there are some rules you are expected to obey. Meals will be provided three times a day and the menu will be of the kind of food eaten in your chosen country. As I mentioned you must attend language lessons which will take place in the mornings. In the afternoons you are free to roam around the grounds, however, you may not pass beyond the gate, but since that is six kilometres away there is plenty of room to explore!

"In this half of the house you may go where you want, but the other half is private and you may not enter. You will see armed guards around the property and that is because our benefactor is a wealthy man who requires security for his personal safety. The guards are here to protect you also, but they will be strict if they find you breaking rules. If the world outside were to find out that you are here then you would be taken away and deported back to Sudan immediately.

"You will be required to attend the surgery regularly for full health screening to ensure that you are not carrying any disease. Hygiene is considered important and so please make sure that you wash daily. Lastly, men and women may talk without restriction, but any sexual contact will be dealt with very harshly, it is not permitted. There is a prayer room on the second floor.

"Please go now to your rooms and we will meet again at supper."

Initially Hani found her accommodation intimidating and she could not relax in the room, which to her delight had an adjoining bathroom, something she had never imagined existed before. The bed was soft, too soft, and there was air conditioning, but circulated cold air was definitely a step too far. She opened the window which had a panoramic view of the bay and faced south, looking back towards her homeland she imagined. A soft breeze blew. She explored the room and in the cupboard was a selection of women's clothes for day and night wear. There were traditional Sudanese dresses, but also some modern European styles. She rummaged through the contents of the wardrobe with a sense of wonder and excitement. She would try on the jeans and T-shirt, but only in the privacy of her own company.

As the days passed she began to feel at peace in the surroundings. She went for walks, at first very timorously, and then with other refugees. She was consoled to hear that they had also felt unsure, but that their apprehensions, like hers, were overcome by the gratitude and trust they placed in Allah.

Each day seemed to bring something new and the days passed rapidly. Apart from language lessons they received tutoring in the geography of Europe and some of its history. Group discussion sessions were undertaken in which they were asked to talk about the politics of their homeland and to outline their personal experiences detailing their own stories and describing why and how they had fled their homes.

Lessons began with learning the Roman alphabet. Tutoring in vocabulary and phonics was gradually supplemented by basic writing. More advanced tutorials focused on how to fill in forms which was considered important. Conversation exercises were endless and there were tests, some of which seemed strange because they used symbols rather than writing, others required them to develop sequences or note the exception in a group. Hani was alert and quick and made rapid progress, to the obvious pleasure of her instructors.

Gradually, friendship groups formed, almost exclusively between members of the same sex. In the afternoons they began to wander further afield and walks in the woods were extended. Hani made friends with a young woman of about her own age, Nadia. They both shared an interest in music. Nadia played the lute and Hani took to the clarinet, which had similarities to the shehnai, an instrument she had played at home.

The only unpleasant aspect of life was the medical examinations they were required to undergo. It seemed that every aspect of their health was studied and they were measured intensively for fitness and physical well-being. Numerous blood tests were required and they were examined inside and out, which included being passed for a long time through a noisy large doughnut shaped machine. Every aspect of their anatomy and physiology was investigated. They were all instructed to improve their physical fitness and were informed this would be measured weekly. A prize would be awarded to the student who made the most progress and Hani was delighted when she won in week four.

One day three members of the original group were absent, but no reason was ever given for their disappearance. The whole group had been together relaxing the evening before, and there had been no indication of a departure, but then they disappeared overnight to be replaced by three new refugees whose journey to Crete had been similar to theirs.

The weeks passed pleasantly for Hani. The more she learned about England and the life of a primary school teacher the more she looked forward to her new life. She was a very diligent student and made increasingly good progress.

As the year turned from early to late autumn they were all asked to help with the olive harvest. Without exception they enjoyed the physically demanding work.

The women placed special nets or big pieces of synthetic fabric under the trees to collect the olives that dropped. The men operated the mechanical harvesters which consisted of a portable generator and a T-shaped rod with elastic sticks attached to it. The head of the rod rotated fast and the elastic sticks hit the olives and threw them onto the nets under the trees where the women collected them. On some days the mechanical harvesters were not available and the traditional way of harvesting was employed with long wooden sticks that were used to hit the olives.

Harvesting started early in the morning and lasted until late afternoon with a noon break for lunch, and so classroom lessons were suspended on the days they were working outside. At the end of the day the full sacks were taken away, to mills for processing they assumed. All the young people thoroughly enjoyed the time spent in the fields which was full of fun, freedom and laughter.

Hani settled into the rhythm of her new life contentedly. The only disappointment was the prohibition on contacting her family. She desperately wanted to talk to her parents, hear their voices and reassure them that she was safe and well. She wanted to tell of her good fortune and excitement about the future, but it had been made absolutely clear that contact with the outside world was proscribed until after they had left the camp. Mobile phones had been confiscated.

Week by week members of the original group began to leave. They were never given the opportunity to have a parting conversation and the remainers were told that their friends' papers had come through. They were now on the way to a new life. Happy news.

Hani had been on the island for just over three and a half months when she was awoken one morning and told her papers had arrived and she would be leaving immediately. She wanted to say goodbye to Nadia, but was informed this was not possible. She was allowed to pack the clothes she wanted to take with her before being taken to a car and driven away. She left behind a very happy period of her life and her apprehensions began to return.

She was driven forever upwards into the mountains until, at last, they began to descend, finally onto a plain that was almost flat and across which they continued for another long while. They drove past endless fields, some with small holdings and others mechanised, until another range of mountains was directly ahead. There were a multitude of windmills in the fields she noticed. At last, they drew up outside what looked like a guardhouse. There was a word written on the gate and calling upon the phonics she had learned she formed the word 'Lasithi'. Papers were shown and the car passed through the gate heading towards an enormous complex. Finally, it pulled up at the base of the mountain.

The door was opened by the driver who escorted her into a building where she was greeted by a woman wearing a white uniform and who chatted away in a language that Hani did not understand. The nurse, if that was what she was, took Hani to a room where she was left to wait and where she found a plate of food waiting for her, she had not eaten that day. Hani was totally compliant and it never occurred to her that she might be in danger.

After a while an older man arrived, grey haired,

slightly stooped and sporting a bright pullover over which he wore a white coat. There was a stethoscope hanging around his neck. He spoke Arabic reasonably well and introduced himself as Doctor Wójcik. He was obviously concerned to help her relax and make her feel at ease. She asked him if her journey to England was now imminent.

"That is due soon," he told her, "but we have a complication. You have had numerous medical tests and I fear that one of them has shown up a condition that means you are not fit enough to travel just yet. Please don't overreact, but we have detected a small growth in the left side of your brain and it needs to be removed. It is not malignant and it is only a small operation which has an almost one hundred percent success rate. So that you may continue your journey as soon as possible we have booked an operating theatre for tomorrow. We anticipate that it will take a week for you to recover and then you will be fit and well. Do you have any questions for me?"

Hani was nonplussed. She felt fit and well and had not experienced any headaches or symptoms, but she could not argue. She concluded that she had to trust the doctor, but she felt small, vulnerable, lonely and more scared than at any time before.

"I have written you up for a sedative that will help you to relax and sleep tonight. You are in very safe hands and so please try not to be anxious."

A strong sedative was prepared and taken in to her by the nurse who stayed and held her hand until she had finished the mixture. Unbeknown to Hani she was being monitored by a small camera high up on the wall that kept watch silently and without blinking while she cried herself to sleep.

In the morning she was woken by the nurse who came into the room and chattered away copiously. Hani understood that she was to take a shower and that she was not allowed to drink or eat. She was given a gown to wear that was tied with tapes at the back, also a dressing gown and she was allowed to replace her hijab. A cannula was inserted into the back of the wrist on her left hand. Hani was compliant and uncomplaining.

When the nurse had left, Hani unrolled her mat and prepared herself for morning prayer. She repeated her gratitude for all the support and help Allah had extended to her and she begged him to look after her father and mother. She accepted that if she needed an operation then this was His will, but she hoped that He would look kindly upon her and ensure she recovered quickly so that she could serve Him ever more diligently in whatever task He wanted her to undertake in future. She asked that He look benevolently upon the friends she had made, especially Nadia, and she expressed the hope that her country could be helped to become a place of peace.

She remained still, praying, until she heard the door open gently and when she turned there was the Arabic speaking doctor with a wheelchair. He came and knelt beside her and whispered, "Insha Allah", to which she intoned, "Insha Allah, Allahu Akbar".

As he helped her into the wheelchair he told her great news. Her benefactor had decided that as she had been through so many trials already he was going to have her flown to England, she would not have to walk across Europe. Furthermore, he had found accommodation for her in a place called Enfield. The doctor took from his pocket a picture of what he told her would be her apartment and which had on the reverse photographs of each of the rooms. She looked in wonder and continued staring with joy at the images as they set off with him pushing her in the chair.

She had expected it to be a short journey to the operating theatre but they seemed to walk for an age down a labyrinth of corridors all looking the same. She was distracted by thoughts of arriving in England and the life she would have working with young children. Perhaps one day she would have a husband and a child of her own that she would bring up in this most beautiful of houses where she would soon be making a home.

At last they turned right and passed through double swing doors into a room that was painted white. There was a gurney in the centre and the doctor indicated that she should mount the small step, sit on the trolley and lie flat on her back. Around the walls were a number of low cupboards and drawers and on one was a kidney dish with a syringe filled with a translucent liquid. In bustled a man who spoke rapidly to her doctor in a language she did not understand. The new man was not particularly tall, middle aged and dressed in 'scrubs' with a cap like a turban wrapped round his head. Most of his features were covered by a mask, but she was fascinated by the profusion of hair that grew in the lower part of his ears and which also seemed to sprout from his nose.

"This is Doctor Iyengar," said her friend. "His nickname is Icarus, but he does not speak Arabic so he does not know I am telling you this." He smiled at her and said, "He does not like the nickname and so you must keep this little secret please."

Hani smiled at this intimacy and she felt her apprehension diminish slightly.

"Relax," he said. "I promise I will hold your hand until you are asleep and I shall be here beside you when you wake." She squeezed his hand.

Dr Iyengar picked up the syringe and inserted it into the cannula.

Her friend said to her, "I bet you can't count aloud to ten before you go to sleep."

She saw the fluid beginning to flow into her arm and as she reached number three there was a rushing sound in her ears and she experienced a sensation of being pulled into a tunnel with increasing speed.

"OK. She is under," said Wójcik. "What a pity. She is a lovely looking woman, both intelligent and sensitive according to the records. She excelled in all the tests and activities. She is in superb physical shape."

"Don't be sentimental," replied Doctor Iyengar.

"Wheel her into the theatre. This is your first time assisting me, I need total concentration."

Under the large triple lights above the operating table, and with the assistance of an anaesthetist and a nurse the operation was begun.

"First we must ensure that she is placed in a permanent vegetative state. There must be no cognisance or evidence of consciousness. For this we shall drill small holes in her cranium and inject an agent that paralyses the function of key areas. We shall leave the cerebellum and brain stem but all four lobes, hippocampus and amygdala must be neutralised. The brain stem tests that we shall undertake must demonstrate that the central nervous system is still active, but that no conscious activity is taking place. Nurse Agnes will then drain her blood to be replaced with oxygen-carrying fluid to ensure the organs remain healthy from the air pumped into her lungs. Nutrient will be supplied directly into her stomach. She must be catheterised please.

"I shall need your assistance particularly for the most difficult and delicate part of the operation, Wójcik. We will make the first incision to gain access to the pituitary gland at the base of the brain behind the nose. Then we will connect these tubes to all the other organs of the endocrine system, which will be stimulated at a maximised rate to produce the hormones we require. Research shows that in the right conditions a body can remain productive for seven years."

The doctors worked for over three and a half hours. Then, when they were satisfied, Hani's body was lifted gently into a case designed to fit her exact measurements. Hinged on one side, it could be closed with vital tubes positioned precisely to allow the ingress and egress of essential fluids. Lastly the temperature of the 'suit' was reduced to the point where her body would continue to exist without deterioration. At face height there was a transparent screen that allowed Hani's head, face and shoulders to be observed. No one had noticed or cared that still tightly folded in her hand was a piece of paper containing her last dream. The casket in which she was placed was then transported to a room in which were identical units, upright like statues connected to individual life support systems. Finally, the lights were turned off.

PART SEVEN

Dino

Stavros Papadakis had been an able boy at school in Heraklion, Crete, where he had spent his childhood. Aged eighteen he applied to read Economics at the *National and Kapodistrian University* in Athens where he was accepted as an academic scholar. Following graduation, he chose to accept the offer of a postgraduate grant to undertake an MSc in *Finance Theory*. Established in 1837 the *National and Kapodistrian University* is the oldest seat of learning in modern Greece and in 1978 Stavros was one of the first graduates of the new Department of Economics. The university has four campuses spread across the city, each in a different neighbourhood. The Faculty of Economics and Business is centrally located in Athens with the main building a few streets away from the Archaeological Museum that Stavros visited regularly to pursue an interest that had begun when he was a boy.

As a child Stavros had often visited the ruins of Knossos, the ceremonial and political centre of the Minoan civilisation, and had been captivated by its history. The ruins were first discovered in the eighteen-eighties and partially restored by Arthur Evans in the early years of the twentieth century. The reconstruction brought the remains of the ancient city alive for an impressionable boy wandering around the site, one whose imagination was vivid and played free rein. Particularly he lived in hope of finding an entrance to the mythical labyrinth where Theseus had defeated the Minotaur and Ariadne awaited his return. There was always a ball of string in his pocket just in case.

At the conclusion of his second undergraduate year Stavros had the opportunity to move to London as part of an exchange programme where he studied at the *London School of Economics*. Here he found himself mixing in a far more cosmopolitan environment than he had experienced in Athens and he made connections with students from around the world, particularly from America. Greatly influenced by the economist John Maynard Keynes, whose book the *General Theory of Employment, Interest and Money*, had featured at the centre of his Master's thesis, Stavros was determined to visit the United States when his studies were completed. He was keen to develop a better understanding of the ways in which Keynesian economics operated in the economy of the US.

He returned from London to Athens to complete his degree and graduated a year later *summa cum laude*. He applied for and was offered a scholarship to study for a doctorate at the Massachusetts Institute of Technology in Cambridge, Boston, and it was here that he first met his future wife, Elena, a very able and attractive Greek student. He also met Aristotle Minas and the two men established a firm friendship.

Stavros and Elena were married at about the same time as Aristotle and Gina and the four mixed socially on a regular basis. Their sons were born within two months of each other and the parents chose names that related back to characters from ancient Greece, an area of shared interest they had discovered. Stavros and Elena called their son Dino after the god Dionysus while Aristotle and Gina settled on Andro, short for Androgeous the name of the son of the legendary King Minas of Crete.

This was a happy time in the lives of both families and the men spent many hours talking about the future and dreaming how they might contribute to making a better world for their children to inherit.

Following completion of his PhD Doctor Stavros Papadakis was recruited by Goldman Sachs as an investment banker and it was as an investor that he was approached by Aristotle to help fund a new and revolutionary drug that he was bringing to market. Stavros was so impressed by the potential of the product that he raised the capital independently from Goldman Sachs, and between them they formed a company, Minas Industries, which launched to enormous success. They created a partnership that was to make them wealthier than they had ever hoped or expected.

The *Enosis* or union of Greece to include the mainland and islands had incorporated Crete in 1913. An administrative reform of 1987 divided Crete into four regional units, subdivided into twenty-four municipalities. At the time that Stavros and Aristotle were searching for a base to establish their production centre one of the four regions of Crete, Lasithi, named after a plateau that lies in the centre of the island, was offering generous tax concessions. Knowing the island well the two men agreed to base their nascent organisation in the Lasithi region of Crete.

It took over a year to build the factory on the Lasithi plateau. The exact site was important and considerable expense was incurred overcoming numerous engineering challenges, and this slowed progress.

When launched the drug was an instant success. In a short time, the factory could not meet demand. Stavros went to work again and rapidly generated enough interest to fund the next stage of development. Production doubled, quadrupled and doubled again. Within a decade there would be factories on every continent, but these were early days and the two families bought houses near one another; one in Agios Nikolaos and the other in Elounda a few miles along the coast. They met regularly and the boys grew up treating each other as brothers.

Elena was a superstitious woman and when Dino was two years old she commissioned a horoscope from an astrologer of the highest repute. He required an enormous amount of detail and it took him three months to complete. When Elena received the final chart and twenty pages of accompanying notes she was excited to find out what the future held for her darling son.

As a baby born in May, Dino was born under the sign of Taurus, the bull. The horoscope foretold that Dino would be reliable, patient, practical and responsible, but also stubborn, possessive and uncompromising. Slightly more worrying was the implication that her son's temperament might not cope well with sudden change or complications that thwarted him, and there was a suggestion that he would experience a level of insecurity manifested in violent outbursts. His extremely competitive personality could be provoked into uncontrolled outbursts of anger unless he learned to manage his temper. He would have the propensity to harbour grudges and be vengeful towards those who crossed him. These characteristics would ensure he became a highly successful man, one who would be fond of money and power which he would wield absolutely. While generally pleased Elena did not show her friend Gina the horoscope and hid it away in a drawer.

The demands of building a business as complex as Minas Industries were time consuming and so Stavros and Aristotle often stayed during the week on the plateau in a comfortable, shared house they had built in Plati, a small village near the offices, and from where they commuted home at weekends. From time to time Elena would accompany Stavros to the house at Plati so that they could spend a few days alone together. On these occasions Dino would stay with the Minas family.

Returning to Agios Nikolaos one icy Friday evening, Stavros made an unwise choice and took a precipitous short-cut along a steep mountain road that snaked between the mountains before descending to the coast. On one of the hairpin bends that traversed a steep gorge Stavros misjudged the width of the track and the offside rear wheel lost traction. Gently but inevitably, and as if in slow motion, the car was drawn sideways and fell onto its side. With the momentum created by the slip it began to roll gradually gaining speed until it reached the edge of a precipice from where it was launched into a void. It took three days before the missing vehicle was found and there were no survivors.

Many years later Dino would have a chapel dedicated to his parents erected at the exact place where it was agreed the car had left the road.

Aristotle and Gina adopted Dino and he became a cherished member of their family. Dino retained a residual memory of his mother and father, but this image of his parents always remained ill-defined, better preserved in photographs than in recollection.

Dino and Andro were brought up as brothers, treated as equals and received the same love and encouragement. When the boys were aged ten a daughter was born to Gina. Ariadne was named after the daughter of King Minas, sister of Androgeous. The boys disdained any association with a baby girl, but were protective of her and grew to be possessive, albeit in different ways.

Aged seven, Dino and Andro were enrolled at a preparatory school in England. Aristotle wanted them to have a British education and he undertook a great deal of research to find a school where an enlightened curriculum was on offer, one that would give opportunity and develop their individual talents. In his opinion too many schools sought to curb individuality and original thought, but in Cambridge he found a boarding school where he hoped the boys would be happy and thrive.

Both boys flourished in an environment that offered academic rigour within a broad curriculum. Andro was a talented musician who took up both the violin and clarinet, while Dino excelled on the sports field representing the school in all main sports. In class they were both considered above average with Dino achieving slightly better grades. They shared a fascination with classical studies and an eagerly awaited period in the week was the listening to myths and legends from ancient Greece told by their history master. In time Homer and Virgil were studied in depth and their imaginations were excited by the stories of gods and heroes, most of whom were exceptionally violent. Their end of term reports were pleasing, although occasional remarks from the headmaster hinted at some underlying issues: *"Dino deserves praise for his enthusiasm and commitment, but in some relationships he is yet to learn to distinguish between encouragement and intimidation".*

There was one incident that was never reported officially to his parents, but it caused consternation. Dino narrowly avoided expulsion and had there been any evidence his school career would have ended in England. He was in his last year and as a thirteen-year-old adolescent his body had begun to lay down muscle. Dino had been introduced to boxing by an enthusiastic PE master and as a pugilist he was assiduous in his training regime and strong for his age. A boy called Peter Middleton complained that Dino had stolen from his tuckbox and following an uncomfortable conversation with the headmaster Dino was known to have been simmering with resentment and anger. Later that day Peter was found unconscious in the grounds and one of his fingernails had been ripped off, when he fell it was assumed. There was a whiff of suspicion, but no evidence and none of the staff wanted to believe that Peter's situation had been anything other than an accident.

Both boys passed to Harrow School with excellent results, indeed Dino was awarded the Beckwith Scholarship, a highly respected distinction. Although putative brothers they had decided to take places in different Houses, their choices reflecting their differing interests. At the conclusion of the first year Dino was nominated for a number of awards and it was clear to the 'Beaks' that he had the potential to be an outstanding pupil.

As if to complement his achievements in the classroom Dino also developed as a formidable athlete. He was not exceptionally tall, under six foot, but he was compact with unusual upper body strength and he excelled on the rugby field, as well as in athletics and hockey. Soccer was not a game that interested him greatly and while he played cricket with precision the game was not one of his passions. The sport, though, that he continued to pursue obsessively was boxing, just at a time when it was falling out of favour in independent schools. However, there was an underground movement that sought out boys with talent in the ring and arranged for them to fight away from school and Dino was approached to join the group.

The fights he enjoyed were mostly not the sport of

gentlemen, undertaken according to the Queensbury Rules, rather they were little more than bare-knuckle street fights, some of which resulted in brutal injuries and a visit to hospital for one of the contenders. Considerable wagers were laid and much emotion was engendered in the crowds that attended. Dino did not fight for money but for the endorphin high that suffused his body when he stood over his bloodied opponent. He had a curious style and adopted a stance with his arms tucked around his head. Some wag nicknamed him 'The Bull', a sobriquet that stuck and was apposite for he literally charged his opponents and beat them into submission with a combination of skill and force. As he became older and stronger fewer boxers were prepared to fight him so formidable was his reputation.

Andro also progressed a hobby that became a passion. Having attended a course of instruction that introduced him to scuba diving he took every opportunity to become better qualified and he regularly joined dives in lakes, rivers and at sea. From his first dive he was captivated by exploration of the underwater world and when back in Crete during the holidays he joined a club that took him to reefs off the coast where he started to visit and explore offshore wrecks.

Andro's most subversive activity was playing clarinet in a jazz club. He thoroughly looked forward to the evenings when he could escape the shackles of school and immerse himself in the music, riffing and extemporising in the heady, smoky, underground world. This was the limit of his teenage rebellion and all that it took to satisfy his deepest yearning was the atmosphere of a club and the appreciation of the audience, both of which were deeply satisfying.

Throughout the years of their education the boys returned home for each vacation. Particularly in summer months weeks of freedom in the sun, sailing and exploring the island developed in both a deep love for Crete. Aristotle allowed them the freedom to pursue interests according to their temperament and personality, but always harbouring the hope that they would choose to become involved in the family firm. He would take them to visit the company complex at Lasithi and spent time talking to them of his passion for the business he and Stavros had created. As they became older he arranged for them to have work experience in the factory during the long summer holiday.

The reports that Aristotle received of the boys' engagement and application at work pleased him. Dino seemed the more driven and ambitious of the two, but he was occasionally fierce and coldly imperious; traits that would have to be managed Aristotle informed Dino. If he was provoked his temper would flare. Although he learned to impose discipline upon his emotions Aristotle worried that Dino also learned to mask his true instincts.

There was one instance when a red neck of an employee accused Dino of being overbearing and 'acting like a dick'. Thereafter the same man regularly niggled him about his spoilt lifestyle and privileged, pampered existence. It was Dino's first encounter with a Marxist-Leninist, one who truly did look forward to the day of revolution when the bourgeoisie capitalists, the cancer of society, would be replaced by true socialists. The bullying continued for too long. Sensibly Dino remained controlled and managed the situation with a mature disdain, but this only seemed to provoke the man further. On Dino's last day before returning to school, the man was found unconscious with five bones broken in his right wrist, which would mean that he would not work for some weeks. The man had no recollection of what happened and his employers concluded that he must have been careless.

Dino was accepted to read Natural Sciences at St John's College, Cambridge while Andro gained entry to St John's College, Oxford to read Classics. During their Oxbridge years the boys grew into young men. Both developed their interests and enjoyed the different environment of their universities. For Dino the ascetic world of Cambridge suited his personality and his focus became the award of a first class degree at graduation. For Andro the more intellectually liberal world of Oxford was a good choice and he thrived in an environment where he became increasingly politically aware and interested in bringing about philanthropic social change to improve the lot of the poor and dispossessed. He would frequent the Union and was a regular contributor to debates. A 'neo liberal' according to a jibe from Dino.

Following graduation Dino was accepted on a doctorate programme at Harvard to research for a

PhD in bio-chemistry and he moved to the United States. Andro chose to stay in England and was taken up by PricewaterhouseCoopers to train as an accountant.

Aristotle continued to work quietly in the background hoping to inspire the boys to take an interest in the family firm in the hope that they would join the vast organisation that was now Minas Industries. For him they were its future.

Harvard in Cambridge, Massachusetts, suited Dino admirably. His research in the field of endocrinal gene therapy was deeply satisfying and started him down a road of thought and experimentation that would lead, ultimately, to his adaptation of Myalycin into a new variant of the original, although he was initially unaware of this direction. The focus of his research took a dramatic turn when he met and spent many hours talking with Philip Stevens, a brilliant physicist at MIT, the Massachusetts Institute of Technology, also in Cambridge, Boston. Philip was exploring the effect of proton and neutron streams on certain molecular structures. He espoused his belief that the centuries old dream of the alchemist might be achievable, although with enzymes and proteins rather than metals.

Medical research has always been at the cutting edge of innovation and the new field of genetic engineering was being pioneered at MIT and Harvard at just the time that Dino and Philip were beginning to discuss their ideas. These were to lead to a radical new approach in drug creation that combined their disciplines, although, as yet, neither was aware.

An intense relationship developed between Dino and Philip who became lovers. Their intellectual, political, philosophical and physical orbits coincided and a very bright flame burned between them. Dino came to believe that he had met the person through whom he could focus all his emotional needs and the two moved into an apartment that Aristotle had bought for Dino.

Returning a day early from a symposium in Chicago, Dino arrived home at their apartment to hear noises from the bedroom. Listening to the two voices, he established what was taking place and Philip was definitely involved. Dino left the flat and only returned when expected the following day making no mention of his discovery. Tragically, the following weekend when Philip was driving home a tyre blew just as he entered the gate of the railway level crossing, trapping him moments before a locomotive bore down on the unfortunate car and its driver who had been unable to escape. The locking mechanism of his seat belt had jammed. The wreckage was so widespread that only parts of Philip's body were found for burial.

Dino was devastated and experienced a complete mental meltdown. For some reason that no one could establish he fled to Bolivia to make a complete break with Harvard and his memories of Philip. There he lived in poverty and squalor for two months earning money to feed a growing drug addiction. It took

Aristotle two months to trace Dino and then to make arrangements to fly to Sucre, one of Bolivia's two capital cities. When he found Dino, Aristotle was shocked at the sight of the drug-ridden wreck of a son he found living in desperate poverty. Dino was taken into care and flown back to the USA where he received the best attention money could buy at the Betty Ford Clinic.

Gradually, Dino returned from the dark world into which he had descended. With time and patience, he came to realise that he risked jeopardising his future and he returned to Boston to complete his doctorate before moving to Athens. He started experimenting and refining the ideas that he and Philip had discussed at such length in another life.

Aristotle observed the young man carefully and began to be reassured that Dino's devils were behind him. He expanded Dino's remit and was relieved that the two brothers worked supportively of each other without any sign of rivalry. Gradually, the young men began to rise up the corporate ladder in parallel. Their skills complemented each other and Aristotle held the secret hope that when the time came for him to retire the two would be ready to take over the company and build upon his success, but then tragedy struck, Andro was killed in a diving accident.

Andro was an expert diver who was scrupulous about safety, however the coroner ruled that the cause of his demise was 'death by misadventure', a tragic accident. Forensic evidence showed that when Andro switched from main to reserve tank he was poisoned. Because of an unexplainable mistake the safety tank had been filled with nitrogen and not air. How or why this fatal mistake happened, or who was responsible, was never established. Aristotle and Gina were devastated. In fact, Gina never fully recovered emotionally from the death of her darling son.

Ariadne was sixteen when her brother died. She had always been close to Andro and his death destabilised her. She returned home to be with her parents and stayed for a few weeks. During this difficult and desperate period Dino came to view his sister differently. When he analysed his feelings he realised that she was becoming a woman and a clever, interesting one at that. He began to pay her more attention and gradually she came to appreciate the support he gave her.

Two years later when her time at school came to an end Ariadne returned to Crete to live at home and Dino set out to court her. He made her feel very special; he took her to places she had never visited and introduced her to ideas, music and literature that she had never experienced. He took her to cities of culture and showed her houses of couture where they mixed with the elite and lived the lifestyle of the international jet set. As she became ever more sophisticated she grew into an impressive young woman and he was proud to show her off. Intellectually strong and physically very attractive she gained the confidence and independence required to launch herself into the same world. Dino flew her to exciting exotic cities and introduced her to famous sites of historical and archaeological interest, and with his refined, urbane ways he made her feel special, wanted and desired.

Within eighteen months of her leaving school they were married and Aristotle was delighted that a dynasty was being forged, one that would ensure his legacy and continue the company that he had spent his career creating.

But underneath the surface there were cracks in the relationship. While Dino expressed devotion he became increasingly cold towards Ariadne and rarely came to her bed. He would spend long periods away and never explained where he had been, or with whom, and he began to drink to excess. When drunk he was abusive towards her and once accused her of sleeping with a friend of his; he slapped her with such force that she fell and cracked her head. One day she found some white powder wrapped in a small paper package in his desk drawer and she confronted him with the evidence. He agreed to seek help again and she announced that she intended to move to England for a time while he recovered. She had been offered a place at Jesus College, Oxford to read for a degree in English Literature. She began to realise that the foundations of her marriage were insubstantial.

What Ariadne could not know was that Dino had exaggerated his reliance upon drink and drugs to cover another life, one that took him to some strange and dangerous places. It suited him to disappear for a while and for this reason he agreed to her suggestion for therapy. However, Ariadne was his wife and he was determined that she would be subservient to his will so that together they would create an heir worthy of inheriting Minas Industries. Her decision to move to England came as a complete surprise to him and at first he considered breaking her will and forbidding her act of rebellion, but Aristotle supported his daughter and Dino did not want to destabilise his relationship with her father.

As the economic crisis in Greece had begun to escalate Minas Industries had looked to diversify its interests and one of Dino's initiatives was to set up a new division offering security services. This proved successful and profitable, especially in the sphere of surveillance. Ariadne may be in another country but Dino followed her activities with microscopic interest. When she met Professor Thomas Miller he was determined to find out more about the man who was screwing his wife.

PART EIGHT

Aristotle

Aristotle could always remember the exact moment. He was seated in the Wolfson lecture theatre in the Department of Chemistry at Harvard listening in a half-hearted way to a thoroughly dreary lecture. The hall is steeply raked so that one looks down on those in the rows below and because the seating is on a curve if you look at a forty-five-degree angle it is possible to observe the whole profile of a person sitting, offset, in the row below, as long as they are not too close to anyone else. She was on her own. Her legs were crossed and her elbow was balanced on her left knee with her head cupped in her hand. A look of concentration made her look as though she were frowning.

Her dark, thick, lustrous hair was cut to collar level and was swept back; it was held in place by her large dark glasses to prevent it from falling across her face. She had a small retroussé nose and freckles that complemented her skin which glowed with youth. Her mouth curved upwards giving her a look of continuous good humour. There was an allure to her face that captivated him. While most students wore jeans and T-shirts, affecting an air of insouciance, she dressed in complete contrast. The month was May and she had chosen a summer frock in bright colours, rather in the style of the 1950s. The bodice hugged her chest and constrained an impressive cleavage while the skirt flared from her hips and he could imagine that it created a provocative wiggle when she walked given the high heels she was wearing. He observed her in minute detail and in a state of wondrous rapture.

At the conclusion of the lecture he hoped to catch up with her and introduce himself but his route was blocked and the last he saw of her was a shapely calf in high heels disappearing out of the door. In those few moments Aristotle's world had changed.

Son of a moderately successful shipping magnate, Aristotle had enjoyed a comfortable childhood. At school he was prodigiously bright and had developed a fascination for chemistry when an inspiring teacher demonstrated that the subject was capable of producing magical results, at least for a boy with an active imagination, and so it was no surprise that he chose to pursue this interest. He returned top grades throughout his school career and his father suggested to him that if he wanted to study the subject seriously then he could do no better than attend a university in America. He applied for a place at Harvard and his parents were both delighted and proud when an offer came through.

His epiphany took place early in his third year and left him bereft. He may never see her again or even have the chance to talk to her. But he was a Greek and so he offered up a prayer to all the gods who might look favourably upon him, and they responded for two days later he was having coffee in a parlour when she and a girlfriend entered chatting animatedly and sat at a table nearby. This time she was wearing a light, close-fitting pullover with a high rolled neck tucked into a pleated skirt that clung to her body and highlighted her transfixing shape. But how to effect a casual encounter and not make a complete fool of himself? First he had to find out some facts: her name, her address and whether she was in a relationship. When he saw her stand and leave in advance of her friend, he rudely sat himself opposite the girl and asked as many questions as he could think of. Fortunately, the girlfriend had a sense of humour and was prepared to indulge this lovestruck swain. She told him that the name of his inamorata was Gina, she was in her first year, reading chemistry and her parents lived outside Chicago. She was most certainly in a relationship and could not be prised away from Tony.

Aristotle was taken by surprise at his obsession. For the following days he could not think coherently and thoughts of her reduced his capacity to function. As he awoke there she was in the forefront of his mind and when he wanted to go to sleep it was her image that prevented him. When he was concentrating upon his studies his thoughts, without invitation, would segue into images of her. He was disappointed in himself because he had an ordered mind and was meticulous in the organisation of his life, or at least he had been before this chaos started.

It took Aristotle four months to create a plan, put

it into operation and propose marriage, and a further three months for Gina to fall in love with him. When she did it was with conviction and a profound sense of gratitude to whichever deity had pointed him in her direction. Aristotle graduated with a good degree and their wedding was a grand affair on a Greek island dedicated to giving the couple the best possible start in life.

Their early married life was a whirl of social engagements, parties, soirees and events for they were a celebrated couple, a popular, charming and attractive addition to any social gathering. Aristotle's parents had bought them a house in Boston and, while Gina chose to complete her degree, his first appointment was as a research chemist with Glaxo Wellcome, which proved interesting and rewarding employment.

As they settled into the routine of married life Aristotle focused upon his research with increasing application. At some stage a novel hypothesis had formed in his mind and he felt convinced it could lead to a radically new methodology in drug formulation. It took some months of experimentation to tease out what it was that was unique and to develop a new research paradigm. As he experimented further the more sure he became that he could make a major breakthrough in the realm of biological science. However, to do so raised for him a profound ethical problem. If he was correct the drugs that followed would make a fortune for the company, but little more than an acknowledgement in his case, and it was for this reason that he compromised his integrity by submitting false data.

When he was sure that his breakthrough was based on robust and secure results he discussed with Gina what to do. He explained to her that the course of action he was considering was essentially illegal and he would never work in the pharmaceutical industry again once it was known why he had left the company. On the other hand, this should be balanced against the fabulous riches they would enjoy if he could prove his theory and bring the product to market. Gina asked for two days to consider the matter as the ramifications of the choices were so profound. In fact, she raised the subject the following evening by asking him what sort of investment would be required to bring the drug to market readiness and start production. The answer flabbergasted her. It was Gina's idea that Aristotle sit down with their good friend Stavros Papadakis in whom she was prepared to place trust.

And so it was that Aristotle resigned his position and with the support of Stavros was able to rent a sophisticated laboratory with the equipment and support required to progress his work. The results exceeded expectation and once the safety tests proved efficacy without risk to health there was no impediment to progress. Not one of the peer reviews undertaken, however stringent, showed any significant cause for concern and permission was granted to undertake human trials. Aristotle took care to disguise the formula as he did not wish any competitor to emulate the composition. Glaxo took out an injunction against him claiming breach of contract. Their case was that the new product belonged to them under the terms of misappropriated intellectual property, but he was able to establish to the satisfaction of the court that his breakthrough came after he had resigned.

Stavros rode the wave of media interest and investment flowed into the new company enabling them to commission a design for a production facility that would match demand. The human trials were given a clean bill of health and a licence was granted, which meant that Myalycin could be sold on the open market.

Aristotle told Gina that the new factory was to be built on Crete.

Gina did not speak Greek and had never left her home country, but neither of these were impediments to a move and she set about planning their new life in Crete with ruthless efficiency. Her only conditions were that she would visit the US as regularly as she wished and her parents could visit Crete equally frequently. The fact that Elena and Stavros would live nearby was an important factor in helping her to settle to the idea.

By the time that Elena and Gina had organised their new homes on the coast of Crete they were both pregnant and the excitement of incipient parenthood offset any of Gina's or Elena's concerns. The fact that Aristotle and Stavros were away on the plateau so much of the time was the only grievance the girls expressed and Aristotle, particularly, missed Gina. He persuaded Stavros to allow some of their investment funding to be used to build a very comfortable house that both couples could use near a small village called 'Plati', a few miles from the site of the rapidly emerging complex. The two women made the journey up to Plati regularly and the relationship between them grew ever closer. These were busy and happy times for both couples.

The arrival of their sons changed the domestic routine for both families and the women visited Plati less regularly, although they grew even closer and the boys were as brothers almost from birth.

Choosing a name for their child caused a slight tension as Gina wanted an all American first name and Aristotle was set on Greek provenance. In an attempt to resolve the stalemate one Saturday, a couple of weeks before the birth, Aristotle packed a picnic and took Gina to visit Knossos where he escorted her around the site. He shared with her the stories he had learned so well in his youth and he wove a web of myth and legend. He recounted how the Minoan civilisation had been at the centre of the known world for centuries and explained why the island had become the hub of trade, politics and power. He told her that the greatest of the Minoan kings was Minas who had two children, Androgeous and Ariadne. They agreed that afternoon to name their children after the son and or daughter of this omnipotent king.

When tragedy struck it was a hammer blow, Stavros and Elena so cruelly taken. Of course Aristotle and Gina immediately took Dino into their home and smothered him with love; they could never be his biological parents but they would be the best substitute possible. However, the world had tilted on its axis and their lives would never be the same again. For Gina some of the light went out and for Aristotle it was as though he had been separated from his shadow. Aristotle made the decision to establish a new headquarters for Minas Industries in Athens while leaving laboratories and production on Crete. When the boys went off to school Aristotle and Gina chose to live in the capital city on the mainland, returning to the island only when work required his presence and for the school holidays so that the boys could enjoy the freedom of an uncomplicated life.

Aristotle and Gina were proud of their sons and they arranged their diaries to include regular visits to England where they made numerous and usually unannounced visits to the school to support sports days and matches, concerts, drama events and Speech Days. At first they watched the boys anxiously concerned for any signs of unhappiness. They were desperate that neither should feel any sense of rejection at being sent away to board, but both settled quickly and loved the busy, active life of school. Dino at this time was more reserved than Andro, a little distant and remote, while Andro was like a puppy unaffected by the vagaries of his existence and full of energetic enthusiasm.

When the boys transferred to Harrow from their prep school, Aristotle and Gina again watched carefully, but the transition was smooth and as the years passed they observed with pride the boys' progression from childhood into early manhood. The move to university was another transition and Aristotle and Gina became aware that their influence was diminishing as the two became independent adults perfectly capable of making their way in the world. Aristotle quietly and carefully worked to entice them both back into the family fold.

Aristotle and Gina loved the life of Athens where they had established themselves in the higher echelons of society and mixed with the most powerful and influential in the land. They had a house designed by one of the country's leading architects and built in the fashionable Plaka region of the city. It was a grand residence in every respect with high ceilinged rooms, a large entrance reception and an impressive sweeping staircase that encircled the central atrium of the house.

Aristotle had sensed in the early part of the new century that the Greek economy was becoming vulnerable to various fiscal pressures. These were creating an illusory wave of economic optimism and the country was naively living as if the party would never end.

Aristotle was right to be concerned but he had not appreciated the depth of the underlying weakness of the economy. The root cause of what was to become an economic crisis was debt, not initially government debt but that incurred by Greek households and corporations. After Greece entered the Eurozone, interest rates fell dramatically, not only were rates on loans relatively inexpensive but banks were willing to lend because of the booming economy. However, in less than ten years, private sector debt as a percentage of GDP, more than doubled to well over one hundred percent. Government debt to GDP hovered at a similar level during the same period. The nation was importing more than it was exporting and so creating a huge trade deficit and debt began to accelerate. This was initially compensated for by higher national borrowing. The process spiralled and when the global economy entered into a deep recession Greek households and businesses experienced difficulty repaying their debts. Unemployment grew rapidly and the consequent ballooning government budget deficit resulted in higher public spending and lower tax revenue. In a short time, banks were unable to recapitalise and became bankrupt as international banks and creditors called in loans.

Aristotle had seen the need to diversify and when Andro joined Minas Industries as a qualified chartered accountant a part of his brief was to research industries that would be compatible with, and would bulk up Minas Industries' portfolio. He was given the task of identifying companies that were vulnerable and potentially profitable. Andro persuaded his father to invest in transport, especially in northern Africa, and also technology, which had multiple aspects that could be developed by a company that was quick on its feet to spot emerging trends and commercial need.

Dino joined the company two years after his

brother and he brought expertise in bio-chemistry. When he outlined to Aristotle and Andro his revolutionary breakthrough with Myalycin there was a sense of palpable excitement about the future. Dino asked for and was granted the funds to build a particle accelerator at the site on Crete.

An outsider might have observed that the brothers were close, but in fact there had always been a distance between the two, something that Gina had perceived early on but never mentioned as she was determined to treat them equally. However, she had always known there was a ruthless streak in Dino's nature and she knew that there were times when he had systematically set out to undermine his brother. The signs had been there from an early age. As the frequent object of Dino's unkindness Andro was wary of him and had a fundamental mistrust of his brother's motives.

When Dino first presented his plans for Myalycin 2 to his father Andro decided to investigate. He called upon the services of various experts all of whom were sworn to secrecy, and what he began to discover horrified him. If Dino's proposed activities were ever to be found out it would be the end of Minas Industries and probably indefinite jail terms for all those who had sanctioned the project. He decided not to approach his father but to give Dino the opportunity of withdrawing the project without humiliation.

When they met Andro calmly outlined what he had come to understand, but he was unprepared for the reaction it provoked.

"You have always been spineless, quite incapable

of taking a risk. Under your leadership the company would be as rudderless as the Greek economy. Surely you must understand that what I am proposing offers mankind the greatest and most precious gift ever granted? Not only will Minas Industries occlude even Microsoft and Apple as the greatest and wealthiest company ever created, I am offering you, our family and the business the opportunity to become so influential that we will be consulted by world leaders. We will hold such influence and power that we can be more philanthropic than anyone has ever been before."

"But at what cost, Dino? Are you truly prepared to put your immortal soul at risk?"

"Come off it Andro, the cost is almost non-existent and traded against the good we shall do for all humanity it wouldn't even appear on one of those balance sheets you love so dearly."

"No Dino. I mean human cost, not financial. I cannot countenance what it is that you propose. I may not be a particularly moral person but I know the difference between right and wrong and this is just plain wrong. In fact, it is so wrong that I intend to stop you."

"But surely in your simpering utilitarian heart you must understand that what I propose is right? And before you start telling me there are moral boundaries I know them well enough and that's why I have worked to improve the lot of people in the future. I am the ultimate philanthropist. The point is that my work is morally justifiable and the sacrifice required is minimal. It will never even be noticed. Your lack of moral courage is a weakness that parades as ethical integrity. The moral argument about what I am trying to achieve is not actually about ethics, it is a justification and I am telling you now, we will progress this research."

"Dino. I give you a week to dismantle the experiment before I go to father with my evidence. I know that he will not sanction you to progress any further."

Three days later when scuba diving around a wreck that Andro had been exploring for a few weeks he switched to his safety tank.

Neither Aristotle nor Gina would ever recover from the death of their son. Aristotle reacted with fury. Someone must be responsible for such carelessness and he was determined to track down the individual upon whom he would rain down the retribution of the gods. Such vengeance would be exacted that the poor creature would be destroyed as thoroughly as an insect squashed below his shoe and ground into the dirt. At moments of lucidity he understood that his anger was entirely disproportionate and that it was the manifestation of his despair, it was as if by exterminating the person responsible he could return life to Andro.

Gina, on the other hand, retreated into herself and passed into a place where Aristotle could not reach her. Just at the moment that they needed each other most they travelled in diametrically opposite directions. Their grief was beyond consolation. Although neither parent had ever acknowledged the fact, Andro their natural son was rooted the more deeply in their hearts. Their love, that began at the moment of his birth, had deepened and expanded over the years as they watched him grow from a gentle, somewhat self-effacing little boy into a kind, generous, sensitive young man who was passionate in his desire to leave a mark upon the world. 'To make a difference' was his mantra and the yardstick he used to measure his actions.

They had been so pleased when he met Lydia nearly two years earlier. Gina had watched Lydia and scrutinised her as only a mother can. She was reassured that Lydia truly loved her son and that she would make him happy, between them was a bond that would strengthen and not diminish over the years. Only two weeks before the accident Andro and Lydia had sat with them holding hands and sharing the news that they were engaged and hoped to marry before the end of the year.

Once the funeral was over Aristotle rang the family doctor and asked him to call upon Gina. He fully expected the doctor's report to recommend a holiday, a sleeping pill, and counselling, and he was sure that it would be full of platitudes about time as the great healer, but he was not expecting to receive a request for Gina to attend the hospital to undergo a series of tests.

Gina seemed to age in front of Aristotle's eyes. Her luscious hair turned grey and lost its body. The laughter lines around her eyes became etched into her face and somehow the elasticity of her skin disappeared, as if giving in to a hopeless battle with gravity. If they were going out she would make an effort with make-up to hide the ravages of grief, but only half-heartedly. Of course she had taken Myalycin over many years but the effects were not evidenced in her physiognomy. It was not altogether a surprise when the doctor told Aristotle that Gina was showing the first symptoms of early-onset dementia, probably Alzheimer's.

Dino had proved to be an enormous support. He could not have been more considerate or caring and insisted that his father leave the running of the organisation to him until he felt ready to return. The only light in their bleak existence was the return of Ariadne who came home to be with them for two months. They knew that she was too young to be exposed to the full impact of the tragedy and so they worked hard to disguise the true depth of their misery when she was in the house.

Gradually Aristotle and Gina managed to work out coping strategies and to the outside world at least it seemed as though they were re-establishing some normality. However hard Aristotle searched he could find no evidence as to how the accident had happened and he had no target upon which to fix his outrage and anger, and so he threw himself back into the company full of burning energy.

It was at about this time that he was approached by the Greek government to explore whether he would set up a new highly secret research project at his site on Crete. It was not the kind of facility that sat easily with Aristotle, but he involved himself in the project, devoting his time and energy establishing

Section 31 as it came to be known, and everyone else accepted that they should leave him to it.

When Dino asked for Ariadne's hand in marriage less than two years later, Aristotle and Gina were initially at a loss to know how to respond. Certainly he could not have been a more solicitous son and Ariadne was clearly overwhelmed by his courtship; she was determined to marry. The establishment of a Minas dynasty had great resonance with Aristotle and in a sublime way the union of the two would bring together the families whose lives had been so intertwined for two generations. However, both parents were uneasy in ways they found difficult to articulate but events moved so rapidly that they had to suspend their unspoken concerns devoting themselves to giving their beloved daughter the best day of her life.

Some months later their worst fears were to become a reality and by then Gina was convinced that Dino would only ever make Ariadne unhappy. She asked him to visit her privately and she hoped to persuade him to annul the marriage before it became destructive as it surely would. As a mother she knew her daughter had the capacity to give unconditional love if she were to meet a man who loved her passionately, but with Dino she was trapped in a relationship that would ultimately lead to her destruction.

Dino was curious to know what Gina wanted to discuss and so he agreed to a visit. Gina had made arrangements for the two of them to talk in private and she had carefully prepared the meeting to take place in her private drawing room upstairs in the

Athens house.

"It is a very delicate matter, Dino darling. May I speak openly and honestly without rancour?"

"Of course, Mother dear. There can be no other conversation between us. In what way can I help?"

"I have watched carefully and I don't believe that there is any real love between you and Ariadne, will you consider granting her her freedom? I have spoken with her and she agrees that she rushed into a mistaken marriage. She is very young, far too young to commit to a man she does not love."

The transformation that overcame Dino was extraordinary and she was entirely unprepared for his reaction. He was suddenly suffused with anger and it was unrestrained.

"You are all the same, you bloody Minases. It was the same with your ghastly son, my titular brother, Andro. You all thought of him as the true, good and virtuous son but he was a weak simpleton who deserved what happened to him. Now you think that you can undermine me and ruin what has taken so long in the planning and execution. Well, you cannot."

With that, he stormed out of the room. Gina was distraught. She stood and followed him. As she reached the top of the grand staircase she heard a movement behind her, and that was the last she knew until she awoke in hospital ten days later with no recollection of what had transpired. A nurse brought her a wheelchair, for her neck had been broken and she would never walk again.

PART NINE

Crete

At 08:00 on 20 May 1941, German paratroopers jumped out of dozens of Junkers Ju 52 aircraft across key areas of Crete.

However, the invading blitzkrieg had underestimated a substantial resistance from the local population. Cretan civilians picked off paratroopers in the air or attacked them as they landed with knives, axes, scythes and in some cases even bare hands. As a result, many casualties were inflicted upon the invading German armies during the battle.

This was the first time the Nazis had been met with such ferocious resistance from a local populace, and the people of Crete were to pay a terrible price for their courage. Intense resistance continued throughout the war and the occupying force were to discover that the Cretan people were hardy and brave, but retribution against the population was brutal. The Nazis never managed to extinguish resistance and although the exchanges were ferocious the people were never suppressed. The resistance fighters retreated into the mountains from where they organised many of their activities.

Most of the geology of Crete is constituted of limestone, dolomite, flysch and schist, which form the majority of rock types, but it is limestone that predominates. The mountains that surround the Lasithi plateau are covered by snow in winter and in spring large quantities of meltwater from the Mount Dikteon range flow towards the lowlands. Over aeons a number of large gorges and more than three thousand caves, with numerous underground passages and tunnels, were formed in the mountains, especially in those that surround the Lasithi plain from where the Resistance organised and coordinated many of its efforts.

The interconnected network of caves and tunnels lay dormant after the war until Minas Industries expressed an interest in excavating them to create a large complex of laboratories.

An underground facility suited Minas for the location had the advantage that there was no need to disguise the activities taking place and it was simple to guard against unwanted intrusion. Pharmaceutical espionage has always been ferocious and when Minas embarked upon building his factory he was determined that no other company would infiltrate his campus.

Minas took one further step to tighten security by employing the shepherds who roam the mountains to patrol the hills and report any activity. The indigenous shepherds are extremely hardy and uncompromisingly tough. They are also well armed and have earned their reputation for violence. The griffon vultures that soar in the thermals around Lasithi ensure that all evidence of their 'justice' disappears from the remote, high hills. In effect he created a militia and very few attempts were ever made to approach Minas Industries from the hills, certainly none ever succeeded.

The very extensive production centre where the pharmaceuticals were formulated and packaged before being exported around the globe, was situated on the plain itself and acted as a protective screen between the outside world and the activities that were undertaken underground. The administrative centre of the Minas Industries site lay at the hub of the complex, and it was here that Ariadne was welcomed and ensconced in the office that her father had occupied when he had been based on the island. The executive function of Minas Industries was now located in Athens and Aristotle or Dino only visited the island from time to time.

In the third week of November Ariadne took up her new role as Chief Operations Officer on Crete. Aristotle's instruction to Ariadne had been that she should learn about every aspect of the organisation. There would be one exception, the area known as Section 31 was, for the moment, to remain off limits. He explained that Section 31 was a joint Minas and Greek government project and subject to extreme security. The other thirty sections, though, would all fall under her control. In essence the fifteen sections outside were for manufacturing, while the fifteen underground were dedicated to research and development. Section 31 was a discrete underground unit.

Sections fifteen to twenty were allocated to physicists and would be Thom's working domicile, for this was where he was to join the team that worked with the particle accelerator. As with the project at CERN, the cyclotron had been built in tunnels underground. A large team of physicists, engineers and research assistants had been formed to further scientific understanding of superconductors, including the development of solid hydrogen; but there was equally intense interest in the work that Thom's team had been progressing in Cambridge examining how chemical properties can alter when particles are passed through certain molecules at the speed of light.

At the north-west base of Mount Dikteon, where it meets the almost level plateau, lies a village, although hamlet would be a more appropriate designation, known as Plati. It comprises an unassuming collection of houses similar to many such that are sited on a road leading nowhere. Some of the houses are motley, others have been modernised, but there is no centre to the settlement and the general impression is of dilapidation, a village through which you would drive rather than one where you would stop.

If one were to drive east from Plati, along the low level of the plain, then you would soon arrive at the seemingly endless security fence that surrounds Minas Industries. This fence is fortified, which includes the deployment of some very sophisticated electronic surveillance and deterrence devices. It is extremely unlikely that anyone would attempt to penetrate the cordon, but should they unwisely try they would not progress very far and life would become extremely uncomfortable once taken into custody. Further to the east and beyond the large complex lies the village of Kastelliou, from where numerous tourists drive to the car park at Psychro to make the walk to the Dikteon Cave, otherwise known as *The Birthplace of Zeus*.

Viewed from the air the mountain extends north onto the plain in the shape of a thumb. To the left lies Plati and the right Psychro. Minas Industries extends around the neck of the promontory.

Behind Plati the mountain rises steeply and at an altitude of just over six thousand feet the temperature is comfortable in summer but often harsh in the winter. Hidden in a fold of the mountain and screened by oak trees lies a small mansion. It was built by Aristotle Minas and his partner when they first established Minas Industries and lived on the plateau to oversee the development of their growing empire. Mostly Aristotle's family stayed in the spacious house he had bought near the old port of Agios Nikolaos, but from time to time he brought them with him to the Plati residence. Ariadne remembered these visits with fondness. With eight bedrooms, a large heated swimming pool, spa and a bungalow for servants discretely removed from the house, it was a comfortable and airy dwelling in which Ariadne now took up residence in late November, this being when her appointment as Chief Operations Officer became effective. Her drive to work was no more than twenty minutes.

On arrival in the extremely spacious office that had once been her father's, she was pleased to discover she would be working with a team of able men and women who appeared, at least at first impression, to be thoroughly professional and who welcomed her arrival. There did not seem to be any resentment at what might have appeared to be a nepotistic appointment, indeed she detected a sense of relief that someone very senior from the centre of the organisation would now be in situ. Her Personal Assistant, Nikki, was clearly an able and likeable woman who would help to steer her through the first few tricky weeks until she was settled and accepted for her own merits.

On Ariadne's first morning Nikki had a sheaf of briefing papers for her to read and she took Ariadne through the diary explaining who had been prioritised and why.

"But," said Nikki, "before you go much further I suggest that you meet Georges Papadopolus who is Head of Security. He will introduce you to the site and give you the necessary permissions so that you can move around without hindrance."

As instructed Ariadne stopped at the third door on

the right and looked at the nameplate that announced:

Georges Papadopolus
Head of Security
Lasithi

She knocked and entered.

The man behind the desk rose and said, "Good morning Mrs Minas." He was lean, wiry and stood with military bearing.

"So you know who I am."

"I would not be very good at my job if I did not recognise the daughter and wife of the two men who employ me and who is now our new Chief Operations Officer here at Lasithi," he replied with a wry smile. "Please sit down and tell me how I can be of assistance."

"Well, as I am sure you know my purpose here at Lasithi is to learn about the research and development undertaken by and for Minas Industries. My brief is to audit, investigate and learn about every aspect of the organisation and so my first question is, how good is the security?"

"Perhaps I am not the best person to ask. I am responsible for all the security, and so any answer I give will be biased. If you want complete reassurance then I can only suggest you find an independent expert to audit my systems, Mrs Minas."

"Actually, I find that a reassuring answer. Since I know nothing about security systems I shall put my faith in you. I do know that my father has total confidence and that is good enough for me," Ariadne concluded with a small smile.

"I have a letter here, addressed to you personally, from my father. He authorises you to give me the highest level of clearance that will admit me to all areas of the Lasithi complex."

"At present, Mrs Minas, there are only three people with such authority – myself, your father and Dr Dino Minas."

"Well now there will be four. How long will it take you to prepare a secure card that gives me access to all areas?"

"You will have the card within the hour, but I hope that your father has explained that I cannot allow admission to Section 31."

"Indeed he has. I assume there is no way that a security card can be copied or cloned?"

"The card I shall give you, like all others, is only activated when accompanied by your thumbprint and a unique, six-numeral pin number created by you. There is only one machine in the world that can copy a card processed in this office, which is that one over there. To clone a card would require breaking into this room with a card, pin number and the owner's thumb. Unlikely, I think."

"Thank you, that is all very reassuring. I have one final request. Please let me have a plan of the whole Lasithi complex. I would be very disappointed if I were to discover later that any part had been redacted. Do I make myself clear?"

"Indeed you do, Mrs Minas, and you will have all the plans you request by the end of today. I would like to assure you that you may trust me implicitly and if I can be of any further assistance please don't hesitate to ask. I shall be grateful if you will leave your father's letter with me. For the record you understand."

"Now if you will follow my instructions we shall prepare the security card and then I will show you around the site."

It was a long journey around the production centre, especially as Ariadne had to be introduced to numerous key people. She made extensive notes and would commit names to memory later once she had the time. She asked Nikki to draw up an operations chart with photographs of the key personnel.

The three research and development sections were a different proposition and she postponed those visits until the afternoon. Bio-chemistry lay at the centre of the Minas Corporation activities on Crete and understandably occupied the largest area, flanked by physics and vivisection on either side, not that she saw any evidence of animals. There was also a medical centre with its own operating theatre attached to the unit, which was reserved for staff in the event of an emergency she was informed.

The Head of Bio-chemical Department, Doctor Iyengar, in answer to her questioning was keen to explain that no animal experienced pain and very strict measures were implemented to ensure that international ethical standards were met. Indeed, he claimed that in every inspection across the preceding five years the department had received a clean bill of health.

The three section leaders were responsible for all research and development and in her meeting with them they talked at length about their current products and the new drugs they hoped to bring to market soon. They stressed again the degree to which ethical standards were met and explained the processes that a new drug must pass through before being sent for evaluation and peer review as a potentially marketable product.

The physics department interested her particularly and she expressed her intention to return and find out more about the experiments being undertaken. Doctor Dominic Wójcik, a medical doctor and physicist, said she would be very welcome.

In all discussions her questions were considered penetrating and she allowed little room for prevarication. Specifically, she wanted a list of all products in preparation and this was promised for the following day.

Over the next few days when not trapped in meetings she spent some time walking the corridors in the labyrinth that was Lasithi. A maze, she concluded.

When the product list arrived Ariadne was confused. Noticeably absent from those ready to go into production was any mention of Myalycin 2. She asked for the Head of R&D to visit and discuss the matter.

Abel Engelmann was a gangly six-foot physicist with spectacles and dark wavy hair. He had a very genial face and while Ariadne thought he looked every bit a boffin he seemed too young to hold such a position of responsibility. However, she was soon disabused of her first impression and she quickly came to respect his intelligence.

Ariadne began, "My first question concerns Myalycin 2 which I have been led to believe is at the pre-production stage. I am even sure that I have seen mention of it in some journals, but it does not appear on your list."

"Well that's a difficult one. You see we developed a prototype, but then ran into some problems and so it was recalled. M2, Myalycin 2 that is, is not on the list because we are very near but are not yet satisfied that we are ready to go into full scale production."

"What sort of problems did you run into?"

"Well," said Abel, "M2 involves a radical new concept in medicine. The drug is formed from hormones extracted from the glands of certain animals. Simply put, this extraction is then placed in a particle accelerator and the vibrations created change the properties of the atomic structure which, in turn, alters their valency. What we are creating is a drug that when taken by humans slows the ageing process even more effectively than before. It does this because it inhibits the release of the ageing hormone from the pituitary gland.

The important difference between M1 and M2, as we call them, is that originally the chemistry of M1 was formed entirely through a synthetic process that produced a drug which controlled the flow of testosterone and oestrogen, but now, with M2 we are using refined hormones to interact with the whole endocrinal system. The efficacy is vastly increased by including a small amount of hormone extracted from primates. Our results have shown that, ageing can be slowed dramatically. When we get it right a ten-year course of M2 should extend life expectancy by fifteen years or more."

"So what's gone wrong?"

"Well. When we first experimented on animals the results were spectacular in almost all the species in which we introduced the formula. It was at this stage we went public as an early prelude to marketing the finished product. Unfortunately, when it came to humans the promise we had seen was not repeated and the difference between M1 and M2 was marginal."

"Have you found out why?"

"Well, yes we have. In fact, the breakthrough came when Dr Dino Minas suggested we expose the hormone to molecular change by placing it in our particle accelerator. We have now identified a specific animal hormone that responds appropriately with human anatomy and the early results are proving very hopeful. But there is another problem and it requires getting the proton stream from the particle accelerator adjusted to exactly the right level. As yet we have not cracked this, but we have a top professor from Cambridge coming to work with us and we are optimistic that he will help us solve the final part of the equation."

"Surely it will take years to prove the efficacy? People will have to live a lot longer before anything is proven."

"Well, the marketing campaign, as ever, is designed to promote sales and with M2 the punters have to believe that the drug will fulfil its promise. Without M1 this strategy probably wouldn't work, but given that it is a new improved version of a successful product we anticipate it will sell well, and of course if we get it right the potential sales are stratospheric. Most people, certainly in the first world at least, won't wait years before starting to take it because they will have missed out on the gain, they will want to start what is a systemic treatment immediately. If it is later proved to be quackery, then all they have lost is some money and the company will go bust. But, they will conclude, we would not sell phoney Myalycin as its failure to deliver would destroy the company. In other words, people will buy on faith alone. Belief will have to follow."

"You do realise that the next five years financial modelling of Minas Industries is reliant upon M2 coming to market in the next few months? If there is any doubt or uncertainty our competitors will spread the seeds of doubt and the damage could be irreparable. Can you reassure me that we can go into production in the new year as planned?"

Abel Engelmann left Ariadne deep in thought. Here

was the first test of her ability to manage the company to success. She was sure that her father must know the situation exactly, and he would be watching to assess how she handled this potential crisis.

Following her meeting with Engelmann, Ariadne decided that she must spend more time in the research areas. She walked the corridors and asked endless questions. To her increasing annoyance she could not always get the definitive answers she sought. Which company supplied the hormones for M2 was a mystery. She even tried to find the answer by trawling through the company accounts, but layers of obfuscation defeated her.

She was interested to know which animals had been used for vivisection, but she could find no evidence of animals on site. Again the answers she was given were confusing and equivocal.

She paid attention to the chemistry laboratories and asked endless questions about the composition of M2. When she pursued the provenance of the hormone supply with ever greater determination she was told that this was information restricted to Section 31. A frustrating answer. Increasingly she began to suspect that the apparent openness of the three departments was screening some information they did not want to share with her. However, she did not want her increasing interest to be obvious and so avoided discussing her concerns openly.

Ariadne was also having to ensure that one of the production lines was tooling up to be ready for production of M2 and this required endless discussion. The prototype of M2 submitted to the regulators had passed scrutiny and the factory was now poised for assembly once final authority was granted. The chemical formulation would not change and so resubmission to NICE in the UK and the FDA in the US would not be necessary she was assured. Tests on primates had shown no side effects and there was no instance of harm to humans.

Much now rested on the skill of the new physicist who was needed to ensure the success of the product. Professor Thom Miller was due to arrive in mid-December.

PART TEN

Plati

The British Airways flight from London Heathrow on Friday afternoon began the final stage of its descent into Heraklion and through the oval window on the port side Thom had his first view of Crete, dry and mountainous. The aeroplane flew parallel with the coast before dropping down onto the runway that perched at the edge of the sea.

So much had happened in the last few weeks, and during the flight Thom had allowed his mind the freedom to roam through the tumultuous events that led to his departure from England. For a long while after the funerals he had seemed frozen, incapable of making a decision or operating on a functional level, it was as if his capacity for independent thought and action had been excised. He consciously tried not to think about Angela or Little Tom because when he opened his mind, even a chink, to memories of either or both it was as if a large wave overwhelmed him and he felt as if he was being sucked into a whirlpool of despondency, despair and unhappiness.

Why had Andrew Wilson asked him if the murder of his family could have been an act of revenge? Of course not, for there was no motive. But the suggestion that Thom himself might have been responsible, however indirectly, for the deaths of the two most important people in his life, stuck in his head like a bur that he could not shake loose.

These thoughts had circulated endlessly in the previous weeks and he had not been able to settle to work or at work. It was as if he were caught in a vortex from which there was no escape, even in sleep. He had taken a flat in Cambridge and paid the rent for six months, but he had very few possessions with which to inhabit it and the sterile atmosphere of the place stifled him.

It had taken the best part of six weeks to uncouple his life from Cambridge and to arrive at the point where he could depart unencumbered. Despite the Dean granting indefinite leave Thom would not leave the College without putting his work affairs in order. He had been to stay with Angela's parents but the weight of the collective grief had been too much for them all and he left after two days. He tried retreating to his childhood home, but his mother suffocated him with her love and his father's stoical support assuring him that it was only a matter of time began to infuriate him. Leaving the country for Crete was the only positive action on the horizon.

And then there was Ariadne. He had hardly dared open that door either. Meeting her in Athens had only confused him further. It had seemed so natural to be with her and he had felt comfortable in her company, but he could not escape the sense that he was being disloyal to Angela. This thought was ridiculous he told himself as she was dead, but he was honest enough to admit to himself that he had not experienced guilt about his extra marital affair when she was alive and he still didn't, why not?

When he had left Ariadne in Athens it was as if the pit he was occupying seemed even deeper. She had her life there and while he knew that she still had strong feelings for him, now that he had seen her in her natural environment he knew there could be no place for him; he had been weak when he told her of his feelings. She had understood all along and that was why she had broken the relationship at such an early stage before it became destructive. He had not heard a word from her since they had last spoken in Athens airport where more was left unsaid than was said. She had mentioned that she would be in Crete at some stage, but he knew that she would avoid him, which was for the best. So, as he approached Heraklion his life felt empty and devoid of purpose.

The pilot landed the plane in textbook style with no more than a gentle bump as the wheels bounced on the runway. It was a short taxi for the aeroplane to the small, concrete terminal and the umbilical was quickly attached. The efficient cabin crew had the doors open and were preparing for the turn round before the last passenger had disembarked. The short journey through passport control and luggage collection was swift. He had been informed that a car with satellite navigation could be collected from the Hertz car rental booth in the Arrivals concourse.

Absorbed and with head down he walked through the automatic exit doors. As he looked up to get his bearings there she was giving a small hesitant wave. At that moment it was as if someone had delivered an enormous thump to his solar plexus.

Ariadne had purchased a Toyota Landcruiser, it being one of the few vehicles that could truly and reliably cope with mountain terrain when off road as well as with the exigencies of the Cretan winter weather above the snow line.

As they joined the motorway they maintained an uncomfortable silence. Every time one of them started to speak it coincided with the other and so it seemed that they were continually apologising. In consequence, conversation was hesitant as they progressed east and south for the hour it took to reach their destination. Ariadne decided to keep the banter neutral, pointing out landmarks and giving Thom a tour guide description of the island's sites.

"The Lasithi plateau is famous for the number of wind pumps used to raise water for irrigation. The soil is fertile and the plain is a major agricultural area. The water table is close to the surface and at one time there were more than ten thousand pumps with their distinctive white sails dotted all across the plain, but many were replaced with diesel pumps during the twentieth century. Paradoxically, with climate change and the push for low carbon solutions the old wind-driven pumps are starting to return.

"The plain stretches 6.8 miles east to west and 3.7

miles from north to south and lies at an average altitude of over two thousand feet. Winters can be harsh and snow on the plain and surrounding mountains can persist until mid-spring but we are not expecting snow just yet, although it won't be long. Oh, and the goats climb trees and the griffon vultures have a wing span of up to nine feet."

Finally, they drove through Plati and wended their way to Ariadne's house. "You will have to stay here tonight but there are eight bedrooms, which gives you seven to choose from. We will house hunt tomorrow, although I fear there are few places in the area that will offer the comfort you are used to in England. I have made a simple supper and I hope you will join me."

"That will be lovely," said Thom.

In the end they decided upon a barbecue and while Ariadne prepared a simple salad and boiled some new potatoes, Thom spit-roasted a spatchcock chicken that had been marinated in olive oil and aromatic herbs which Ariadne had collected from the mountainside. By the time the chicken was ready it had turned cold outside and they agreed to eat in the kitchen. Ariadne had bought some local wines and two bottles seemed to disappear easily as their conversation became more relaxed and they eased into one another's company. Ariadne built a log fire in the comfortable den which they agreed was preferable to the spacious but rather grand sitting area. The room quickly became snug and they sat at either end of the long soft-leather sofa, near but apart. Neither acknowledged it but they had slipped into feeling comfortable in the other's company and enjoying the companionship. As they chatted they became more confident in the relationship and even their occasional silences felt more natural.

At last Ariadne decided to take the bull by the horns. "Thom, I have decided to leave Dino. I have told him that I need my freedom. I want him to have the chance for happiness and while I understand his desire to have a Minas child I could not spend the rest of my life waking every morning knowing that I do not love the father of my son or daughter."

"How did he react?"

"It was strange. He looked at me for a moment with so much venom that I wondered if he would become physical again. Do you remember that I told you once there is a shadow over Dino's soul and at that moment something stirred deep inside him, it was intimidating. But he has enormous self-control and whatever it was he was thinking he drew a veil over his true feelings and observed that my future might not work out as I hoped. I didn't quite know how to interpret that, but before I had the chance to discuss the matter he disappeared into his study, a room that is strictly off limits to anyone, and so that was the end of the conversation. I have contacted a solicitor and papers are being prepared."

"What was your father's reaction?"

"It was strange. He said, 'Then I shall have to put measures in place.' I have no idea what he meant."

The hour came to wish each other goodnight, and once again they found themselves clumsily parting, this time for their separate annexe of the house. They agreed to meet for a run before breakfast.

Thom took a while to unpack his clothes and

arrange his travel things in the bathroom. Thoughts of Ariadne were whirling around in his head and he knew that sleep was not imminent. As he drew back the cover of the bed he could not help but find a sheet of paper tucked just below the pillow, it was a copy of the poem she had sent him after Oxford all that time ago.

The sun was shining above the azure horizon by the time Thom and Ariadne met for a cup of coffee before setting off. They ran side by side at a comfortable pace, both enjoying the freedom the exercise granted them. After a relatively short distance they extended their pace and gradually increased speed, matching each other step for step. Their running was not competitive but it was hard, both up and downhill. Thom had no idea of direction and so Ariadne guided him along the mountainside before descending to the plain and continuing around a circuit that brought them back to Plati and the house. By this time they agreed they were ravenously hungry and Ariadne rustled up some bacon and eggs, fresh orange juice and more coffee.

"I need a shower," said Thom.

"Why not a swim? The water in the pool is a heavenly temperature and it would be refreshing."

Neither of them mentioned the poem. Thom thought a swim was a great idea and they went their separate ways to change. Fortunately, Thom had had the foresight to pack a pair of trunks.

Ariadne arrived at the poolside first and, draped in her towel, she sat at the round table by the steps that extended into the water to wait for Thom. He followed soon after and she could see that despite everything that had happened to him over the last few months he had kept himself fit and he was well toned.

She stood and placed the towel over the back of her chair, her hair was tied up. She was wearing a sunshine yellow swimming costume that swept down between her plump breasts and plunged from her hips between her legs. Her modesty was maintained but not by much for the clever design of the swimsuit highlighted every curve of her body in a thoroughly provocative fashion as she walked into the shallow end.

Thom tried and failed to stop himself staring at every contour of her body. As he descended into the water he followed as if in thrall. When she ducked her torso and re-emerged from the water her nipples had come erect. With water up to their waist, they stood facing each other only a couple of feet apart. Deliberately Ariadne extended her arm and stroked his penis. The effect was electric. She undid the tie of his trunks and released him. He leaned forward and slid the straps off her shoulders with the effect that her breasts appeared to balloon out of the costume. He continued to unpeel the swimsuit until it could be discarded, at which point she used the buoyancy of the water to wrap her legs around his waist. She whispered, "We have world enough and time now, my darling."

Later, when they were lying in her bed she asked him if he would forego living in a place of his own to keep her company in this house and in this bedroom in particular.

Much later they began to talk in earnest, and once started they seemed unable to stop. They talked of nothing else but their feelings for each other, it was as if they had to purge themselves of some transgression, as if they had to atone for the time they had been apart.

So began the time they would live together in the house as man and woman. They spoke constantly of their feelings for one another and the mutual fascination that had ignited on that night in Leicester Square. The more they conversed the more they spun a web around themselves forming a cocoon from which they hoped never to emerge. Each in the other found the peace they had been seeking, and so it was that their lives fused, as though they were now welded in a bond that would be unbreakable.

They found that they could disagree without acrimony, they delighted in sharing the smallest task however irksome and they chattered like birds; they were equally content with companionable silence. They introduced each other to music and would sit listening for an age, arms entwined as if drawing strength from the connection. They would make love wherever and whenever the mood took hold of them.

There were times when they caught the other

staring in introspection and if asked they would exchange the moment, happy or sad, giving succour and strength. One minute they could be analysing emotions as critically as a psychiatrist and in the next cavorting like children.

Over the weeks that followed Thom's arrival they came to understand that they were free, liberated and infatuated. What had begun between polar opposites, a romantic and a logician, now transcended the confines of any boundaries, and in this way they entered, subliminally, into a contract that was increasingly resilient.

Angela and Little Tom did not diminish in Thom's mind but they began to recede and he hoped that were it possible he would receive their blessing and they would want to confer happiness upon him. Both Thom and Ariadne had experienced the trauma of loss and bereavement, and the experience acted like a lens bringing focus and intensity to their love for each other and giving clarity to their understanding of what mattered most in their lives.

At times their conversation was frivolous, at others it was searching and complex.

One evening Ariadne said, "Did I tell you about my moonbeams cleric in the church where we listened to the *Messiah*?"

"St James? No, you haven't."

"There was a day when I was in the deepest despair and I went for a walk that took me past our church. I went in and sat in a pew. He came and talked to me and said he had been watching me and that he had made me a cup of tea because I looked so deeply troubled and unhappy. All I could think about that day was losing Petra and you.

"He asked me if my dreams had broken. He said that dreams are like moonbeams you hold in your hand for a while, and he said that our happiness comes to us like a child's bubbles that sparkle and then phut, they shatter and disappear. We cannot hold on to our dreams but through them we have a glimpse of God. He said that if I hold faith with Him, then God will not desert me, the moonshine will come again. My clergyman was full of such simple piety and certainty, he espoused such a secure faith. He quoted a line from a Betjeman poem: *The Maker of the stars and sea who became a Child on earth for me'*. Imagine that. In that moment I knew my love for you had been a gift from God. He gave you to me and I should never have rejected you, even though I did so for the right reasons."

"You sound as though you have found God?"

"What I feel for you, Thom, does not stand up to analysis or fit into one of your categories, it is not even rational, but my love for you has being and your being gives purpose to mine. Is it God given? Well, I think there's more in Heaven and Earth than is dreamed of in Thom's laboratory."

"You underestimate me, my dearest. I have looked for God in my own evidence-based way. He is elusive, but I have not abandoned the path. My starting point is the Cartesian principle of *Cogito Ergo Sum* which is both logical and reasonable. From there I progress to Anselm's ontological argument, which very, very simply put, requires the premise that we cannot imagine anything greater than God. All my work as a physicist makes that argument perfectly acceptable. I can therefore accept the notion of an architect of the universe as an option in which I can believe, because either the universe was designed or it was not and I have no proof either way."

"So, are you saying that God is a fifty-fifty option?"

"At one time I would have disclaimed God entirely but given the perfection of the working model I favour input from a creator. However, the debate is more complex because of the step I think you are proposing, which is the progression from an abstract deity to a personal God. For me this is where everything becomes rocky. I can analyse the evidence, but I don't need faith to reach a conclusion, in fact logic dictates that proof would deny faith. In other words, I can have a belief in God but I don't have to have faith, whereas you have to have faith to support the belief that God cares for you personally."

Ariadne interrupted. "You believe that the perfect universe you admire could have been created by the most perfect thing you can imagine, and you will call that unknown God."

"Exactly, but we can't leave matters there unfortunately because of your need for faith, faith that God cares for you individually. The Church insists that it is only through organised religion that admittance to God is made accessible. Churches of all denominations claim this monopoly and they claim they have proof, the Bible and Koran are examples, but, they tell me, because they can't prove their proof I must have faith. It is only through their intercession they claim that I can be loved by God. That might be acceptable but they go further and state that I must follow the rules they espouse without question, and so I must become subordinate to the church and not directly to God for they claim to interpret His will.

"The problem therefore, it seems to me, is that religion has hijacked God and, unfortunately, religions have a history of being illiberal organisations because they loathe the principle of personal freedom. Leaving aside some of the horrors taking place now or in the past in the name of God, religions are repressive institutions. Women, and gays to name but two would still not be emancipated if the Church in the west had not been forced to change. Most wars are fought in the name of God with each side claiming his mandate. Thoroughly illogical."

Ariadne interrupted, "There is a poem by William Blake, *The Garden of Love*[10]. It seems to say the same as you: *'Thou shalt not writ over the door, And Priests in black gowns, were walking their rounds, And binding with briars, my joys and desires'*. Is that how you view the church?"

"I could not have put it better," said Thom. "I am not averse to the principle of God, I just think that he is not hidden behind the moon and the stars, but is evidenced by the moon and the stars. He can, therefore, be accessed without being mediated through the Church. Did He come down to earth for you and me? Probably not."

---

[10] Refer to Part 15 for the full poem

On another occasion Ariadne asked Thom if he believed in the concept of Good and Evil. "I struggle with this one," she said, "because in the animal kingdom the survival of the fittest is the only principle that applies, *nature red in tooth and claw*, but is that the same for humans? Are the people we call evil, those who act according to their nature without any regard to others? On the other hand, are those who truly want a better world the weak ones who would be destroyed by the strong if the rule of law did not exist? Genocide would be the obvious example where the veneer of civilisation is shown to be so woefully thin."

Thom thought for a while. "As a physicist so much that needs explaining can be expressed in the metaphor of polar opposites, positive and negative, light and dark, humanity and inhumanity, caring and indifference.

"The concept of Good is a man-made construct which, when observed, ensures order and mutual safety. People who are considered Evil are those who act without restraint or according to their own rules and their actions create social disorder. They are therefore a threat because they are indifferent to the harm they cause. Care, compassion and kindness are in opposition to brutality, violence and desolation; one is constructive, the other destructive. Both are found in human society and the principle of justice, as agreed by the majority, ensures that moral boundaries are defined and upheld, but the rule of law is fragile and breaks down. The fight to overcome the forces of destruction is endless."

Ariadne asked, "What about acts of altruism? The

capacity for goodness is surely innate?"

"That idea has long been discussed and the weight of argument is probably against your view because reciprocal self-interest is generally deemed to underpin behaviour that is known as humanitarian."

"So," countered Ariadne, "does that mean that utilitarianism defines goodness, doing good for the greatest number is the best we can be?"

"Let's just say that there are those in the world who seek to make it a better place and want to alleviate suffering, while in polar opposition there are those who do not care about anyone or anything other than themselves and their actions are brutal. There are, therefore, choices to be made and these will define whether a person's actions are good or bad. Personally, I believe that not hurting others is the only right principle by which to live, but while the human condition as we call it has obviously improved, the horrors persist and probably always will because greed seems to be deeply ingrained in human nature. In conclusion, if selflessness is a prerequisite of goodness and if goodness is a quality of love then I must be imbued with love, because Ariadne I adore you so very much." He reached over and pulled her towards him protectively.

Ariadne had bought a Land Rover Defender which she told Thom was for his use. She did not want them to be seen arriving at work together and so they staggered their departure in the mornings and arrived home when work for the day was completed. The first to return had to prepare supper and soon they settled into a routine that became established including shopping at the weekend and a daily run, swim and meal before bed. They were very happy. She may not have attended church but quietly, Ariadne thanked God for the love of a good man.

Winter arrived in the third week of December. The roads were kept open but the plain and surrounding plateau were blanketed with deep drifts of snow. It was as if Plati had become a remote mountain retreat and when the Minas complex was brought to a standstill for Christmas and New Year they were snowbound in the house for a few days. The relationship between Thom and Ariadne ratcheted a further notch as it progressed from the intoxication of first attraction into the beginning of a stable, deep and profound joy in the company of the other.

PART ELEVEN

BoZ

There are two designs of particle accelerator (PA), linear and circular. The one constructed by Minas Industries in the caves of Lasithi was circular and at 360 metres long it was similar in design to that built at the Los Alamos Neutron Science Centre. The accelerated particles are protons and the kinetic energy required is measured at 800 MeV. Such a cyclotron is primarily used for Neutron Materials Research, Proton Radiography, High Energy Neutron Research and Ultra Cold Neutrons, therefore mostly for medical research. As such the Lasithi PA was ideal for the company's medically biased research and also for its other area of research into superconductors.

A particle accelerator is a machine that uses electromagnetic fields to propel charged particles at near to the speed of light in well-defined beams. Large accelerators are used in particle physics as colliders or as synchrotron light sources for the study of condensed matter physics, however smaller PAs are used in a wide variety of applications that include particle therapy for oncological purposes, radioisotope production for medical diagnostics, ion implanters and the manufacture of semiconductors. The best known and highest energy particle accelerator is the Large Hadron Collider at CERN which operates at hundreds of GeVs. By comparison the Lasithi cyclotron was modest, but substantial enough for the purpose it was designed.

On his first morning Thom was introduced to the Chief Engineer responsible for the running of the cyclotron, Dominic Wójcik. Also to the Head of Research Projects, Abel Engelmann and a third member of the team, a medical doctor, Dimitri Iyengar.

First impressions often influence relationships and as Thom was going to have to work in close proximity with these three he observed them keenly. Engelmann was probably in his mid-thirties, tall, gangly, thin faced with heavy framed spectacles and a mop of unruly dark hair; there was a sense of boyish idealism about him.

Iyengar on the other hand was short and plump with thin, receding, light hair cut short and exhibited a quality of intemperance that led Thom to suspect that he would confuse challenge with disobedience. His tongue kept emerging from his lips like a snake's as if he was tasting the world, and his curiously stubby little fingers moved deliberately in contrast to Engelmann's disjointed arm movements. To Thom's amusement Iyengar had a profusion of nasal and ear hair that protruded in thick bushes. Thom thought he might find Iyengar disagreeable.

Wójcik was the oldest of the three: taciturn, grey haired, a little stooped and with an air of weariness. He wore a curiously enigmatic smile that seemed to imply he had seen the best and worst of humanity. His bright waistcoat was a statement of exuberance belied by his demeanour. He only spoke when addressed and then in taut, staccato sentences, certainly not a conversationalist.

Thom detected a professional rather than fraternal respect among the group who obviously knew each other well and exhibited a workmanlike understanding, at least this was how it seemed to Thom as an outsider. He wondered, though, if there were frictions between the men and he determined to observe them carefully. Perhaps they resented his arrival although he did not detect personal animosity. Thom spent his first few days meeting with Engelmann and Wójcik to develop an understanding of exactly what the project was aiming to achieve, what had been accomplished, what impediments were being experienced and what possible solutions had been explored.

Each evening he reported to Ariadne who was fascinated by his simple explanations of the issues they faced and the thumbnail sketches of the people he was working with. She always expressed deep interest and one evening made an enquiry.

"I have met Abel Engelmann and liked him, Wójcik less so, but how close are you to solving the problem that Abel explained to me is impeding M2?"

"We have to work out exactly what concentration of proton beam we need to use if we are to stabilise the molecular structure of the hormone, that is fundamental to the composition of M2. It really won't take very long; of that I am confident. Wójcik is very competent indeed and knows his machine inside out.

"I don't really understand why Dino invited me here as all the team have to do is work through the various bandwidths and experiment with the concentrations until they hit the right combination and then BINGO."

"Are you saying we will be ready to go into production at the beginning of the year?"

"That does not seem overly optimistic."

"Is that a yes? I need to know, Thom. Will we be in a position to go into production at the beginning of the year?"

"OK. I will put my shirt on it. Of course if I am wrong that means you will have to a) buy me a new shirt and b) make me redundant!"

"Oh don't think that you can escape the clutches of a Greek goddess that easily. Once you have solved the easy problem, you can turn your attention to the superconductors. Crack that one, Professor, and you will have a Nobel prize to put in your pocket and I shall be even richer! Then I will marry you and make you my slave."

"I was born to serve, especially one particular Greek goddess. Is it time to mount Olympus?"

"I will ignore that! But Thom, from where are we getting this vital hormone? I have looked for a paper trail and dug deeply but I can't find the answer. I get fobbed off at every turn by Doctor Iyengar who I'm afraid I find a cold fish. I don't get a straight answer and I have the sense that he is dissembling with me. Whenever I ask a question he doesn't like, his answers become ever more equivocal and he hides behind the third amendment of Section 31. What do you think of him and what about Dominic Wójcik?"

Thom pondered for a moment organising his thoughts.

"The preparation we place in the PA each day is brought to me by Wójcik or Iyengar and so I have no idea as to its provenance or composition. My job is merely to measure the effect of what we do to it. I have introduced some new parameters and we are closer to achieving the result you seek. In fact, as I have said, I am confident we shall do so in the very near future, after which you will be able to initiate production.

"Abel is a good man and I find him friendly, but I agree there is something odd about the other two. I sense they are keeping some important information from me and I want to find out what it is. Iyengar is a bit stiff, in fact he appears rather emotionally deficient. He is certainly humourless and I am not sure exactly what he is up to in his lab. Wójcik though is different, he seems preternaturally nervous and conflicted, it is as though he is perpetually worried about something. He snipes at Iyengar and they act like an unhappy married couple."

Ariadne couldn't quite leave the subject alone.

"Something worries me Thom, but I can't quite pin it down. There are aspects to what is going on down in the tunnels of Lasithi that are too steeped in mystery. I still don't understand how we seem to have circumvented the licensing process for M2. Normally, the authorities won't issue a licence until the final formulation has satisfied every test ever thought of, yet we have permission to manufacture before even proving to ourselves the final composition. We must be flying close to the edge with the authorities."

"Well that's a technicality based on whether the version supplied for approval will contain exactly the same constituents as the one that goes to market and it will, so it has been exposed to the full rigour of the regulator. Remember, the difference lies in the new technique being used here. All we are doing is stabilising the structure so it will be perfectly safe for humans, there is no doubt about that. The drug itself has not changed in any fundamental way since it passed the randomised, controlled drug tests and those proved there are no negative consequences when taken by human beings. The efficacy is yet to be demonstrated but this will become obvious once we have controlled the pharmacology.

"I gather that it was Dino who undertook the negotiations with international regulators and if he has convinced them to license then you can push the button for production without having to worry about safety being compromised. As to where the hormone is coming from, now that is an enigma and like you I would be interested in the answer."

Ariadne changed the subject.

"In two weeks the whole site will close for Christmas and New Year. What shall we do?"

"What an odd question, Mrs M. I am anticipating a large fall of snow and we shall be tucked up under our 13 tog duvet for the duration except for occasional forays into the kitchen and cellar to replenish stocks. Does that meet with your approval?"

Ariadne's concerns stuck in Thom's mind, however, over the next few days he found himself considering the work he was undertaking from a more critical perspective. Also, he began to wander around the central research areas with eyes rather more open than previously.

He engaged in long conversations with Iyengar and Wójcik, probing to find out how the project had originated. It was difficult, as Ariadne had said, to elicit anything definite, but he did establish that the principle behind M2 of exposing chemical structures to molecular radiation had come from research first undertaken by Dino Minas, a renowned bio-chemist in his own right. It was Dino who had initially proposed a causal link. His notion that hormones extracted from the endocrinal system in animals could have their state changed by being exposed to particle acceleration had proved a valid theory. He had become convinced that the effectiveness of M1 could be enhanced by passing protons through hormones suspended in a specific catalyst of his devising. Initial results with animals were spectacularly successful, but then it had been realised that the product was unstable and returned to its original state after a relatively short time when given to humans. With Thom's help the team had now taken a mighty leap of synaptic thought and had proved that by varying the velocity of a proton beam the desired effect could be sustained. They were very nearly there.

Thom was curious about Section 31 but any

mention met a wall of hostile silence. Abel had no knowledge of the secret Section and it had never occurred to him to ask. The other two obviously did know what was going on, but refused to answer any questions and made it absolutely clear to Thom that the subject was off limits and there was no discussion to be had.

One conversation stuck in his mind when, over coffee one morning, the subject of medical ethics came up in discussion and although they were discussing what was a fairly neutral aspect Wójcik had become increasingly agitated. He launched into a tirade.

"The problem with western scruples is that soft liberalism results in moral paralysis. Everyone has a right to a moral position, so explain to me whose morality trumps whose? The answer is that western world power claims the moral high ground on the principle of moral equivalence, but this only ever works in favour of those who hold dominion. If the west rejects genetically modified crops but allows people to starve in the third world, then where is the great moral high ground? If the western world ignores genocide because it doesn't want to be embroiled in conflict, then tens of thousands of innocents are condemned to die. If you don't allow gene modification and children continue to suffer from inherited diseases, then what value ethics? If you value profit more than people, then any moral imperative is lost. It is difficult to know where to find moral leadership anymore."

Later Thom tried to unpick what Wójcik had been arguing. Certainly he was a man with a conscience and sense of duty, but there was an anger directed somewhere else. Perhaps his accusation was that western morality has become so defensive of the principle of the right to rights that action directed by conscience is lost amongst all the voices, most of which represent one self-interest or another?

Thom took to exploring the tunnels. He had been told there was over a mile of underground passageways and when he was not otherwise engaged he walked them. They were of uniform diameter, mostly circular and Thom concluded that a tremendous amount of excavation must have been required to create such unanimity of construction, but it was difficult to understand why the effort had been made on such a scale. He took to mentally mapping the corridors and various departments he passed as it would not be difficult to get lost. His observations began to reveal some curiosities. For instance, at the very rear of the site was a door that logic suggested would only open onto solid rock. One afternoon when no one else was around he used his passkey and slipped through the door, which led him into a tunnel, an unlined rough-hewn rock passage with no lighting. He used the torch on his phone to illuminate a way forward and he was led deeper under the mountain. He nearly tripped over some discarded metal objects and on further investigation discovered what was probably hardware left behind by the resistance at the end of the second world war.

After a while he arrived at a solid strong iron gate. His electronic key proved useless and further access was obstinately denied. He made his way back without incident and returned to the main passage.

There was another unexplained curiosity.

Iyengar had been away for the day and Thom took the opportunity to explore the area around the chemistry and anatomy labs. He wanted to see if he could spot any irregularity or inconsistency that might merit further investigation, but there was nothing that sparked his interest or seemed inconsistent with what he would expect to find. At the back of his mind was the question Ariadne had posed, where was the vital hormone processed and stored? The only thing notable therefore was a complete lack of what he would expect to find.

Adjacent to Iyengar's main laboratory was the operating theatre. This was a well-equipped surgical facility, but as Ariadne had commented there was no sign of any animals. At the back of the theatre was a large aluminium cupboard which he noticed was on runners laid parallel to the wall. When he pushed the cabinet it slid sideways easily to reveal an unexpected, hidden door. His passkey would not operate the digital lock which held fast and denied access to a room that was purposefully concealed. Why?

"Dino has asked that I return to Athens to spend Christmas with him and my father," Ariadne said one evening.

Thom felt the disappointment like a physical force. He looked utterly forlorn, disconsolate she thought.

"May I stay in the house? I have been asked to join Angela's parents where we spent a family Christmas in Northumberland last year, but I have refused. My parents also want me to visit them, but I don't want to return to England even if I can't spend Christmas with you."

Ariadne was sitting on the settee. "No. You may not spend Christmas alone in this house, Thom darling, for the simple reason that I shall be here with you. I thought about returning but that led me to think about Christmas without you, and that left me feeling bereft and so I am not going anywhere."

On another evening Thom asked, "Have you any plans of all the Lasithi buildings because if so please bring them home."

"OK. As it happens I have and I will."

"Is there any way I can use your passkey, because if I am to find the answer to your imponderables I need access to the door in the operating theatre that I told you about."

"No. Out of the question, my passkey only works with my fingerprint, but I just might be able to get you a master key if we can gain illicit entry. The problem is we need to find a means of entering without passing through the main entrance and that's an almost impossible task."

The next day it started to snow and they were taken by surprise at how quickly the depth accumulated.

The wood store was full of well-seasoned logs from olive trees and the wood burner was kept well fed during the Christmas and New Year vacation. The days were spent reading, listening to music and walking when the weather permitted. Mostly the sun shone and as long as they kept moving they were warm.

Behind the house the lower slopes of Mount Dikteon climbed at a relatively shallow angle and it was possible to enjoy a long stroll where the trees preserved paths and the snow was not exceptionally deep. They held hands, they threw snowballs and pulled one another on the sledge before returning downhill tired but exhilarated. Each evening they continued the pattern of taking it in turns to cook, sharing the preparation and the creation of food, occupying the same space and lightly touching as they moved around the kitchen. Their love making was at times unrestrained and at others gentle and rhythmical; at Thom's suggestion Albinoni's oboe concerto became a prelude and accompaniment to their passion. They found contentment living in each other's presence. They were happy in each other's company when they awoke and at the end of the day; the two of them removed from the world and in their own realm, balanced in a state of equilibrium, like twins in a womb.

On the penultimate day of their sojourn, Ariadne announced that she must drive to the office and collect some required reading for meetings that were in the diary for the morning of her return from holiday. Thom suggested that they explore the mystery of the door that led nowhere and perhaps her master key might just unlock the gate he had described to her. It would not be possible to investigate the operating theatre further as security staff were patrolling.

The main roads had been kept clear and were almost empty of traffic. They were welcomed at the main gates and having entered the building they quickly gained entrance to the labyrinth of passages that led them ultimately to the door at the far end of the maze.

"I hope you know your way out of here," joked Ariadne.

"Of course I do. I am an expert in string theory, Ariadne," quipped Thom.

"Ha ha, Thomas Miller. Remind me, why do I love you? Certainly not for your sense of humour!"

Walking at a brisk pace it took about a quarter of an hour to arrive at Thom's mysterious door. He had been watching to see if their progress was being monitored by the omnipresent cameras, but these had become more sparsely positioned as they penetrated further. They passed what Thom had previously established was the last camera and it was situated some distance from their destination.

Ariadne was as curious as Thom who had brought a bright torch with him to illuminate their progress once they passed through the first portal. Opening the first lock was straightforward as before, but the question remained what would happen when they reached the gate. Disappointment. Ariadne's master key proved useless as there was no digital pad or evidence of an electronic lock. Thom gave the gate a thorough shake but it did not budge. There was no sign as to what was holding it tightly shut, perhaps it had been welded?

That evening, their interest thoroughly piqued, they discussed their failure and Ariadne said that she would talk to Georges Papadopolus, but Thom counselled her to step warily as it would seem curious if she were thought to be snooping.

Thom awoke the next morning, the last day of the Christmas break, and something was niggling away at the back of his conscious mind. Ariadne was still asleep and he lay in bed trying to analyse what it was that he had missed the previous day. Analysis was one of his strengths and he was sure he would work the problem through. Suddenly, he sat upright knowing he had the answer. Ariadne stirred.

"There can be only one solution and we missed it," announced Thom.

"What?" said Ariadne sleepily.

"Despite the fact that we looked there must have been a key hole! In which case there must be a key."

Later that day they once again stood in front of the gate. Thom scratched and poked the ironwork of the solid iron postern and sure enough with perseverance he identified a shape that had been cleverly concealed and painted over so that it was not immediately obvious.

"If there is a keyhole then there must be a key."

"That's all very well but we have no idea where to look," said Ariadne.

"Hmmm. I have a theory though. The only purpose for a gate here is to obstruct further progress down this passage in both directions, now why would anyone want to do that? I suspect that this is more of an exit than an entry, perhaps some kind of escape in the event of danger in the tunnels, this area is riddled with interconnecting caves. The strange thing is that back in the tunnel there are no fire escape signs which leads me to think that when someone made that door they wanted to keep this a secret. Either that or it has been completely overlooked and forgotten, but I bet there is a key hidden somewhere nearby because otherwise it would have to be smuggled in past security and their scanning systems."

It did not take long to locate the key as it was perched on a ledge just above eye level. It was a heavy steel key and it clearly had not been handled for a long time. It was covered with the rusty patina that only develops over time and with lack of use. The key slipped exactly into the lock and although stiff it turned relatively smoothly. The hinges needed oiling, but the gate swung open without great difficulty.

Together they stepped through and the chill was immediately noticeable. Thom pointed the torch and they stepped forwards along the passage for another few yards before there was a sharp turn to the right. As they stepped around the corner they nearly stumbled into what was clearly a lake. More than a pond but not extensive, it took them by surprise. There were what looked like stepping stones and it was only when Thom moved the light around that they realised they were surrounded by stalagmites, some of which had broken off just above water level. They looked up, and above them hung mighty stalactites.

"Look at the size of those, they must be at least ten thousand years old," whispered Thom in awe.

Ariadne looked up and far above her she could make out a large opening that from this distance seemed to her to take on the shape of a vagina, as seen by a baby before its emergence into the world she thought. In a moment of comprehension, she recognised where they were, "The birthplace of Zeus. Thom, we are standing at the pool where Rhea gave birth to her sixth son."

"Tell me about the Dikteon cave," said Thom later that evening.

"According to Hesiod's *Theogony*, the first gods at

the beginning of the world were Uranus, the Sky, and Gaia, the Earth. Uranus was fearful of losing his power to his descendants and so cast his children into the depths of the earth.

"Gaia hid her son Cronus from her husband Uranus and later helped him to overthrow his father. According to myth, and on Gaia's advice, Cronus took a sickle and castrated his father Uranus, throwing his genitals into the sea. Thus was born the beautiful goddess of love Aphrodite. Cronus married Rhea but was terrified he would share his father's fate as it was prophesised that he also would be killed by one of his sons. Afraid because of the curse, he swallowed his first five children at birth so they would not be able to usurp him. When Rhea's sixth child, Zeus, was conceived, Rhea was determined that he would survive.

"Rhea asked for help from her parents, Uranus and Gaia. Following their advice, she travelled to Crete and hid in a cave on Mount Dikteon, the one we were in today, to bring forth the child in secret and hidden from her child-eating husband. Throughout the birth, the entrance to the cave was guarded by the legendary Curetes.

"As soon as Rhea gave birth to Zeus, she gave him to Curetes to look after. The healthy boy was to become the Father of the Gods of Olympus, but in order to deceive her husband Cronus, Rhea gave him a stone wrapped in swaddling clothes instead of the baby. He swallowed the supposed infant at once and relaxed once more in the certainty that his life was not at risk from his child. They were not a pleasant group of gods!"

"I must say that I prefer the modern ones and given that you have enslaved this mortal it is only you I worship!"

She ignored this quip. "But from our point of view this is ideal. It is a bit of a stride but we can walk to the entrance of the cave from here. From there it is about one hundred metres down to the lake, but very conveniently steps have been constructed and as long as we visit at night we now have a backdoor into the Lasithi complex."

Thom and Ariadne made their plans carefully. There was nothing they could do until the snow melted which meant they had a few weeks to draw up a carefully worked scheme. They spent hours poring over the site drawings to familiarise themselves with the layout.

As soon as the weather permitted Ariadne took Thom for his first visit to the Dikteon, or Psychro cave, via the entrance. From the car park they walked up the steep path fashioned centuries earlier by the pilgrims who visited the shrine. It was formed of stones like very large cobbles, that were slippery where wet and wound up the hill zigzagging at acute angles. Some were broken and the path was so inclined that it required a concentrated effort to ascend without pausing for a break. From the path were uninterrupted views across the plain and Thom was surprised at how flat the landscape was when viewed from this height.

The path was flanked on both sides by ubiquitous, stunted olive trees, all rather wizened and from a distance they resembled the hunched witches of childhood fable, or so Thom thought.

The entrance to the cave is a large oval hole shaped like an open mouth, and within a few yards Thom saw they were faced with a vertiginous descent, now made easy by concrete steps and a handrail. For the public's illumination green lighting was bathing the cave, and this only enhanced Thom's previous thought, bringing to mind images of a witch's cavern.

Ariadne kept up a running commentary.

"How all those Greeks managed to get down to the pool without killing themselves I cannot imagine, but they did so to make votive offerings on an altar they created at the side of the pool. As we descend you will see pock marks on some of the stalactites, those were made by bullets as iconoclastic freedom fighters shot them for the fun of it, they were amused to see them collapse. Ten thousand years to form and then barbarically destroyed. A tragedy."

Thom lost count of the steps at about two hundred. Some were covered in a glossy coating that looked slimy, and was in fact calcified limestone. Thom was grateful for the rail to hold onto because the steps looked glassy. The chill was constant and the magical effect of descending between the monstrous columns and grotesque pillars was mesmerising.

Once they had descended to the level of the lake Thom orientated himself and worked out where they must have been standing when on the other side.

They had emerged around a very tight corner just to the right of where he was standing; it was impossible to see the passage because of a fold in the rock, the tunnel being invisible from where they were presently orientated. As to how deep was the water in the lake Thom had no idea. One look and the stygian blackness of the water made him quail at the thought of falling in, but fortunately there was a ledge that Thom thought he would be able to traverse if it were not too slippery.

The enterprise passed without incident and they proved to their satisfaction that they could reach the gate and gain entry into Lasithi.

The climb to the surface seemed long and as they emerged from the darkness Thom took a long draught of fresh air to revive his spirits.

As the weather warmed they walked across the hill at weekends and navigated their way to the entrance of the cave which, as the crow flies, was only about three kilometres. They repeated this journey a number of times until they felt confident that they could manage the route at night. Thom drove rudimentary stakes with a reflective marking into the ground every half kilometre along the route for them to follow.

Finally, they settled on a Sunday in late February as the date to undertake their escapade. According to the long-range forecast the snow would have begun to melt and the following day was a Bank Holiday, therefore activity in the tunnels would be at a minimum. The guards might even be partaking of some illicit carousing, which Ariadne knew tended to take place at festival times. How to disguise themselves from recognition when in the complex took some thought and planning. In the end they decided white coats, wellington boots and a headscarf for Ariadne with a balaclava for Thom would have to do. They scoured the internet and purchased two realistic masks that would not immediately arouse concern if the CCTV was only being watched casually. No one was suspecting unorthodox activity and there should be no evidence of their visit following their departure. The key was not to draw attention to themselves. Ariadne established that the local shepherds would not be patrolling the hillside as there was a carnival in town.

It was a cold evening on the designated night and it took them two hours to cover the distance to the mouth of the cave. The descent into the cave was straightforward but the balancing act required to traverse around the edge of the pool was, once again, terrifying. Thom went first while Ariadne pointed the torch, they were joined by a rope in case either fell into the water. Maintaining balance while at the same time imagining that the malevolent pool wanted to suck him in was as much as Thom could manage and his relief at reaching the far side safely was tangible. Their overheated imaginations caused each to falter at one stage and when they were both across they had to cling to each other for support for some minutes. Unlocking the gate was easy and Thom sprayed some oil on the hinges. The digital pad on the door back into the tunnel lit red momentarily but then blinked green allowing them smooth access into the passageway beyond.

"Now remember as we pass a camera keep talking to me and gesticulating as if we are colleagues," said Thom. "The CCTV must not cause alarm."

It was about three o'clock in the morning when Ariadne and Thom stood outside the door of Georges Papadopolus' office.

"The guards do not patrol this building at night because there is only one entrance and there are two armed soldiers posted there all night so we should be uninterrupted," Thom reassured Ariadne.

As they stood in front of the door to their destination Ariadne passed her security card across the reader; at the same time, she pressed her thumb against the pad to the right of the door. She then entered her pin number. The door opened smoothly and because there were no windows Thom felt safe turning on the overhead light.

Ariadne steered Thom towards a small handheld contraption that was sitting on a cupboard on one side of the room where it was recharging. The small machine resembled those used to verify credit and debit card payments. In this case there were two slots, one for an original card and the other for a copy which started as a blank piece of specially treated plastic. The surface of the blank card was covered with a unique polymer only recognised by every reader on the Lasithi site and without which no lock would open. The blanks were kept in a drawer from which Ariadne extracted a single card. She replaced it with a useless replica that she put at the bottom of the pack.

She mimicked exactly the actions that Georges had followed when he created her original. She inputted the pin he had asked her to create and on this occasion she applied Thom's thumb to complete the process.

A small light flashed on the machine and there was a quiet whirr as the card was printed and then ejected. Ariadne withdrew her original and took the new card to another door on the other side of the room to test their work. She instructed Thom to place his thumb on the door pad while holding the copy in his other hand up against the reader. When required he typed in her pin and the door clicked open. It worked.

They made sure that all was as they had found it and left silently, pulling the door firmly shut behind them.

As the door closed a hidden camera switched off. A record was entered in the electronic security log.

Georges Papadopolus' daily routine began with a quick trawl through the daily security log to check for any anomalies. He was surprised to see that the system which presided over his office was showing an entry soon after three o'clock in the morning. He called up the CCTV record and watched what had taken place during the night. Puzzled, he thought for a while before deciding upon what action to take. After a while he reached for the handset of his encrypted telephone.

PART TWELVE

Labyrinth

"What are you reading?" asked Thom.

"*The Poetics* by Aristotle."

"Daddy?"

"No, you idiot, the philosopher."

"Is it a good read?"

"Aristotle was the first to make a distinction between Tragedy and Comedy. Comedy, he said, is about the weaknesses of people while Tragedy concerns a noble person who makes a wrong choice that brings about their destruction. Pity and fear. Pity for him or her and fear for ourselves. Will our choices lead us to our destruction, Thom?"

"How morose, why the melancholy? Take my advice and read a good bodice ripper rather than dull literary theory."

"I don't know, I have had a sense of foreboding all day. Are we too content, Thom? The ancient gods would have resented our happiness; they would have taken it away from us. Remember those lines we used to discuss? 'Things fall apart; the centre cannot hold – about suffering they were never wrong'. What does our future hold? Will we be unhappy?"

"Well," said Thom, pacing around the room, "since I have become your pupil I have come to understand that when you talk about looking beyond the stars you are seeking that existence which lies outside of yourself, it is the infinite with which you connect. In my love for you I know I have found something to which I cannot ascribe an explanation other than it has a beauty of its own. Beauty I suggest, therefore, lies in the infinite, which means it is a constant, it is not circumscribed. So love and beauty are the same thing and they encapsulate all that is good and right in the world. I never thought love could be like that, but now I do. Before falling in love with you I would have said that ultimately everything can only be measured according to its existence in the actual world, but now I have begun to distinguish between the physical and the ineffable. I do like that word."

He continued. "So your distinctions of comedy and tragedy, life and death are only relevant if you seek to catalogue as I have always done, but now I begin to comprehend what you have shown me, which is that the boundaries don't matter. We must look up and out as well as down and within because we are a part of the infinite, therefore whatever happens to us, my love, is infinite." He looked at her and said, "You are beautiful."

"So," Thom concluded, "in response to your challenge I have been reading some poetry. I am rather taken with the one that begins: 'How do I love thee? Let me count the ways'[11]. I have started my list and look forward to reading yours."

Ariadne responded immediately, "'And wilt thou have me fashion into speech the love I bear thee, finding words enough'? Sonnet 13. Oh Thom, I wonder if you know how much I love you, I cannot imagine life without you. Promise me that you will never leave."

Thom was standing behind the sofa and he bent down to wrap her in his arms. As the smell of her recently washed hair filled his nostrils with the scent of fields in spring he looked over her shoulder and read her words:

To have loved and lost comes at a cost.

Better not at all, but that's a call

I could not make, even for the Almighty's sake.

Never since has He granted me a glimpse

Of that which lies behind the veil, only in our tale,

Where all beauty He creates is manifest in your grace,

His deeper purpose now clear, you are close and near

Ever present, hidden in all that is bidden.

"That's truly beautiful," he said. "I want you to know though that I am not a complete Philistine. I have been trawling through your thesaurus to describe my feelings for you adequately. As my ideal woman you are ineffable pulchritude personified, my

---

[11] 'Songs from the Portuguese', Sonnet 43 – see Part 15

Aphrodite. How's that?"

"Well, kind sir, like any goddess worth her salt I am indeed delighted to be placed upon a pedestal, now come here and worship at my altar. On your knees, mortal."

At 10.32am the next day Thom was surprised to receive an email from the Operations Director requesting his immediate presence. When he arrived at her office Nikki greeted him with her usual efficiency and rang through to inform Ariadne of his arrival.

"Are you enjoying Crete, Professor?"

"I am sure that when the summer gets here it will be more interesting. To be honest I am buried underground most of the time and I need to get out more."

"Well I shall just have to rescue you and show you the island and its attractions in all their glory," she flirted in very good English.

Nikki escorted Thom to the Chief of Operations' office with heels that tapped efficiently like a typewriter against the floor. Thom was reminded of being summoned to see the headmaster when at school. He hesitated for a moment before entering when Nikki ushered him in.

As the door closed behind him Thom joked, "Your secretary just chatted me up, we must have made a good job of hiding our relationship because not much slips past that one."

However, when he looked across the room his genial mood changed to one of concern for she was ashen and had obviously been crying. He strode to her side and she rose, clinging to him, sobbing. When she had calmed he elicited that Aristotle had called to inform her that her mother had died in the night.

"I have booked a flight to Athens for early this afternoon and will be away for about a week," Ariadne told Thom.

"Can I come with you?" he asked. "I will remain discreetly out of the way."

"No Thom, I shall stay with Father and it is not the time to tell him about us just yet. He loved Mummy so much despite all that has happened, and I must care for him for a few days while he needs me.

"Also, Dino has written to me returning the divorce papers and I need to have a showdown with him. I must escape his chains. So stay here and wait for me to return, which will be soon my darling, I promise."

Thom made an excuse to be out of the office that afternoon and insisted upon driving Ariadne to the airport at Heraklion.

At the departure gate they held their embrace for a long time, as if they needed to be prised apart. At last Ariadne slipped out of his arms and said, "I'll be back as soon as I can, I promise. Don't go chatting up my PA, she is mine and is not for sharing. Goodbye my darling." Thom was left gazing after her until she disappeared into the melee and was absorbed into the crowd.

When Ariadne arrived in Athens she immediately hailed a taxi and was driven to her father's house in Plaka. Using her key, she let herself in and found him sitting in his study staring blankly into space. As always he was well dressed and well-groomed and it occurred to her that he was still handsome. Aristotle held on to her embrace practically as long as Thom had earlier that afternoon; they spent the rest of the day in each other's company giving and gaining strength. Her father explained that Gina had developed pneumonia a few days earlier, and despite receiving treatment, her condition suddenly deteriorated and she had died unexpectedly during the night from a heart failure.

That evening Aristotle was in a nostalgic state of mind, constantly reminiscing about his and Gina's life together. He wanted to share with Ariadne his love for the beautiful, passionate, vivacious and intelligent woman he had married. Father and daughter chatted animatedly recalling happy memories of family life, especially in Crete.

For supper Ariadne prepared a simple platter of cheese and pate and opened a bottle of red wine, after which they settled comfortably in the lavish drawing room Gina had furnished so tastefully. Aristotle said, "I am glad that she is at peace now, the last few years have been a meaningless existence. I am sure that she would have resented living as she did had she been aware of what had happened to her." Father and daughter talked late into the night, gaining solace from each other's company.

The following morning the funeral took place at eleven o'clock and a large number of mourners joined with the family. As Ariadne took her place in the front row she felt a sense of release as she wished her mother a safe journey.

Then, as she relaxed, and as if from nowhere Dino materialised at her side. She should not have been surprised, but he caught her off guard and before she could enquire after his well-being he snarled in a low voice, "I need to see you when this is over." Peremptory and coldly distant, there was no sign of affection or sympathy for her loss, and certainly no apparent sadness for the death of the woman who had brought him up as dearly loved as any son.

Aristotle had planned the funeral carefully and with love in his attention to detail, the result was an uplifting service. The hymns were chosen from Gina's favourites, mainly those with a strong rhythm and an optimistic view of redemption and renewal. The priest who officiated was a benevolent older man who had known Gina before the illness deprived her of her quintessential spark and in his address he spoke with compassion, humour and kindness, but Ariadne longed for the service to be over and she felt an overwhelming sense of relief when at last they wished the last person goodbye and were able to retreat to the security of the house.

"What are you going to do now that this is all over?" Ariadne asked Aristotle.

"I have been looking after myself for some years and so nothing will be very different. I have not talked to you of Martha, but she and I have been close friends for some while now and I am happy in her company. I think it's the same for her and so I imagine that when a suitable time has elapsed we will marry. I want to be with her and she feels the same. My earnest hope is that you will come to like her also.

"Of course I will, Daddy. If she loves you, then I shall love her. We will be friends."

"And what of you, Ariadne my dearest? Clearly you and Dino came unstuck long ago, but he says that he wants to remain married and is desperate to father a Minas child.

You have clearly made an enormous success at Lasithi, every report I receive is full of praise for your management of the plant, and now that you are about to bring M2 to market you are free to return to Athens should you wish. For a long time now it has been my hope that you and Dino will work together to ensure the future of the company."

It was as if a dam broke inside Ariadne, and emotionally drained by the day, she began to talk to Aristotle compulsively about her life since the time of Andro's death. She said that it had taken her two years to come to terms with her brother's death. She explained that at eighteen years old and having had a very protected schooling she was lacking self-knowledge or self-confidence and she had been overwhelmed by Dino. She had confused an infatuation with something more substantive not understanding that she never loved him in any meaningful way. She shared with her father the deep and complete love she now felt for Thom.

Aristotle was silent as she talked and she began to be unsure of his reaction to all that she was recounting, it occurred to her that perhaps she was upsetting him. That was until he put his arm around her shoulder and pulled her towards him, uttering the words she recognised as the benediction he had whispered over her every night when she was a little girl lying in bed preparing for sleep.

They sat close together holding hands for a long time until, at last, Aristotle declared:

"I can hear in your voice how much you love this Thom and I am content that you have found someone whose love brings you peace. He is a lucky man. However, you remain married to Dino and he is a serious impediment to your future happiness. I have watched Dino closely over the last few months and I have concerns about the direction he wants to take Minas Industries. I perceive a shadow in Dino that disguises something he keeps hidden and whatever it is it worries me."

"You are not the first to use that phrase about Dino," said Ariadne.

"Promise me," commanded Aristotle, "that you will recount to me verbatim what is said in your meeting tomorrow."

"Of course."

Ariadne had suggested they meet at Aristotle's house, instead Dino had summoned her to his office for a discussion at mid-morning. When she arrived he made no effort to relate to her on friendly terms. It was clear that he wanted to address with her a vexatious issue, namely the matter of their marriage, and it was also obvious that this was not going to be a meeting between equals. When preparing what she wanted to say it had not occurred to her for one minute that he would oppose a divorce and she had no intention of refusing any condition he might impose, and so his introductory comments took her by surprise.

"Your father gave you to me in marriage. Marriage is for the propagation of children and so I have booked you into a clinic for the day after tomorrow to be artificially inseminated with semen I have already supplied. You will return from Crete immediately and I suggest that you live with your father for the present as it would be inconvenient for you to return to the house where we were happy before your infidelity and temporary absence from our marriage. Should you not accept my proposition then let me assure you that all you hold dear will be under threat. Please do not make the mistake of underestimating me."

"This is outrageous, we are not living in the Middle Ages, how dare you threaten me? Apart from anything else Father will never allow this."

Dino looked at Ariadne with an unwavering stare and said, "Already you are making the mistake of underestimating me. When M2 is launched in a few weeks then your father will cease to hold the controlling share of Minas Industries. He is an impotent, old man. The sooner he dies and leaves the running of the company to me the better."

"Do you really think for one moment that I shall agree to this sordid proposition? There is nothing on this earth, Dino, that would or could persuade me to return to you and your disgusting sham of a marriage."

"To be honest my dear I don't really care that much, but I want you to have a chance to accept. I am a forgiving man and am prepared to forego your indiscretions, but only on my terms. Please let me have your decision by the end of the week."

"You may have it now. Over my dead body will I agree to your terms. I will have a divorce."

Thom could see from the online diary they all shared that Iyengar was due to be away for three days attending a conference on animal research. Once Thom had established that Dimitri was not on site he thought that maybe the opportunity had arrived for him to explore behind the hidden door in the operating theatre; the best time of day being after all the technicians had left for the day. That morning Wójcik had reported in sick and Abel Engelmann had taken the afternoon off to compensate for some of the overtime he had worked recently. Thom thought he would never find a better moment to explore and in his pocket was the master key he and Ariadne had so adroitly created.

Before leaving his office Thom sent a text to Ariadne, "Going to investigate the labyrinth," that being their reference for the secret tunnel Thom was convinced lay behind the operating theatre.

As he approached Thom checked the location of the CCTV cameras to ensure he would not be observed, but there were none in the operating theatre itself, and he could not detect any in the bio-tech department through which he had to pass. The closest was the one that stood watch over the outer door to the unit and, therefore, once he was inside he would not be viewed.

As he entered the empty department Thom was surprised to note that his body was experiencing signs of heightened anxiety or apprehension; his breathing was deeper than usual, his heart rate had risen and he could sense adrenaline coursing through his veins resulting in a level of hypersensitivity. His rational brain considered the reaction surprising since he was not anticipating that he would encounter any danger.

The operating theatre was sparklingly clean and bright, light reflected off the aluminium cupboards, equipment and work surfaces. Thom walked quickly to the cupboard and rolled it sideways on its track to reveal the door, which was wide enough to admit an operating trolley. He held his cloned key up to the unit, placed his thumb on the pad and typed in his pin code when instructed. There was a moment of hesitation before the lock clicked open and with a gentle push allowed Thom entry. He stepped into a short passageway that was also well lit, and at the other end of which was an elevator with sliding doors similar to those in hospitals. He slid the cupboard back into place before closing the door behind him. He noted that he would need the card again to summon the elevator and once more the duplicate master worked easily. When the lift arrived he saw that there were only two levels and it was clear that he had to descend; he was surprised at how long it took before the lift slowed and stopped. He exited into another airlock and straight ahead of him there was a further door to bar his way, once again the card granted him entry. He would never have been able to progress without the master key Ariadne had so cleverly copied. As he opened the door rows of fluorescent lights flickered on and illuminated a sight that made him gasp.

Ariadne was too shaken to return directly to Aristotle and she wandered through a local park in a daze. At some point she sat on one of the benches and tried to make sense of what Dino had said.

She was confused. She had known for a good while that Dino was a driven man, obsessive in numerous ways, but she had never considered him dangerous, and yet just now he had been the most frightening person she had ever met, her erstwhile husband and brother. Could he really have meant what he said? Her only conclusion was that he did, which implied that she might be in danger and so might Thom, even her father. It was clear that Dino knew of her relationship with Thom and she had been left in no doubt that his threats were very real. She must return to her father immediately.

"He has found a way into the crypt."

"It will take me a few hours but I shall be with you soon. Observe the protocol."

Suspended from the ceiling by wires were multiple rows of sarcophagi, all hanging perpendicular in an upright, standing position, although none were quite touching the floor. There were seven to a row and six rows with a further three to one side. These three were empty, the others were all occupied. The close-fitting 'suits' were made from a rigid material, a plastic of some kind, and appeared moulded exactly to the dimensions of the shape they encased. Thom quickly established that each casket had a clear Perspex window revealing the face of an occupant. From the front of every 'suit' protruded a pipe at waist level attached to a collecting bottle with a tap at the base. The rows alternated male and female. As he moved through the rows it was clear that all the incumbents were of African extraction. The tunnel was long and there was space for numerous further rows, ready and awaiting future occupants it seemed.

Once Thom had overcome his initial shock and calmed his nerves he began to investigate further. The first row was all female and each had a nameplate just below the pane that allowed sight of the face within. The first name Thom could make out was 'Hani'.

Each suit was connected to power and Thom could hear the hum of air being pumped, which meant that the bodies within were breathing, or at least air was being pumped into their lungs. Inserted into the neck of each was a drip solution of some kind, probably nutrition, Thom thought. There was also a mechanism to collect bodily waste fluids. Could the occupant be alive? He stared deeply into the open eyes of Hani and waved his hand, but there was no flicker of conscious response. His conclusion was that her central nervous system was operating but only at a basic level. He assumed the others would be in the same condition.

Beside the door was a simple table with two aluminium chairs and for the first time he noticed a filing cabinet. He opened the top drawer and withdrew the file named Hani, which was surprisingly thick. He sat, placed the file on the table and started to flick through the pages. In the first section were charts recording her physical condition and following that extensive notes and records, clearly she had been monitored and measured extensively. The last section was her personal history, but it was written in Greek and so was impenetrable to him.

Thom was concentrating so intensely on what he was reading that he was slow to perceive a small draught of air blowing across the nape of his neck. When his brain did register that something was out of place he was still slow to respond, it was only the spurt of adrenaline suddenly pumped around his body that led him to leap from his chair and swing round adopting a defensive stance. Standing six feet away was Dimitri Iyengar with a large pistol pointed straight at Thom's chest.

"Professor Miller, please do not make the mistake of thinking that I lack proficiency with a firearm. I am in fact an excellent shot. Also, please do not make the further miscalculation of thinking that I would hesitate to use this weapon. Killing you would cause me no anxiety or regret, only inconvenience.

"Now please stand and with your back to the wall extend your arms fully."

Iyengar produced a pair of handcuffs that he slipped expertly over Thom's wrists and each closed with a ratcheting series of clicks. The shackle was securely welded to a short chain and Iyengar padlocked the chain firmly to a stanchion in the wall. Thom was hopelessly fettered.

"I am leaving you with a bottle of water and a bucket so that your basic needs may be attended to. I shall return, but not for some while, I fear. In the meantime, I hope that you do not become too uncomfortable. You may sit or stand, whichever is more restful, but obviously you are unable to leave. It was most unwise of you to investigate areas that do not concern you." He leaned forward and removed both Thom's mobile phone and his passkey from his jacket pocket, and with that he left the room.

Ariadne recounted her meeting with Dino to Aristotle as accurately as she could remember.

"The awful thing is that I believe his threats, I am sure he will set out to do terrible damage to me and anyone close to me if I do not follow his instructions, but I can't let him defeat me, I won't accede to his disgusting demand."

Aristotle was so intensely quiet that Ariadne wondered if he had been listening to her. When she looked up she saw that he was weeping silently and she went to him to hold him in her arms. He wiped his eyes, and at last he spoke.

"I realise now that I have known for too long, but did not want to accept the truth. I have shared with Dino everything that gives my life meaning; my precious daughter, my company, and, I suspect, the life of my son. And now that he is powerful for some perverted reason he wants to destroy us. I did not see this cancer growing, but I have silently suspected for some while that I might be harbouring something dangerous and destructive. The signs have always been there and I chose to ignore them.

"When he was at school there was mention of cruelty, but your mother would not tolerate any such thought. After Andro died I spent a great deal of time and money piecing together what happened and to my relief no evidence led directly to Dino, but there were worrying indications that he could have been implicated. I would not believe that he was complicit in any way in the death of his brother, but now that Dino's grip on the reins of the business has tightened he is revealing his true character and I have made the mistake of allowing myself to be distanced from some major decisions while his control has been growing.

"It was he who formulated M2 as a development of the original and it was he who demonstrated that it was going to be the blockbuster drug of all time and so I relaxed my oversight, but now it seems he is planning a coup d'état. If we are as close to production as you tell me we are, he obviously feels ready to strike and you it seems are first in line.

"From a small boy Dino could never accept opposition and over the years there have been too many stories of people who have crossed him ending up being hurt. So do I believe his threats to you? I don't want to, but we can't take the risk of ignoring him."

"So what do I do?" asked Ariadne quietly.

"We are going to return to Crete and there we shall draw up a plan of action. Please ring your Thom and warn him to be very careful not to put himself in danger. Then call the airport and tell them to prepare the company jet for immediate take off. The flight plan is Athens to Heraklion, a journey of fifty-five minutes. Go and get ready to depart in one and a half hours, it will take me that long to prepare as I must make some phone calls."

Ariadne left her father in his study to do as she had been instructed, but was back in less than ten minutes.

"I can't reach Thom. His phone has been turned off and the airport tell me that Dino left Athens in the company jet for Crete two hours ago, it's not known when it is to return. You could send for it but there are seats on the scheduled evening flight and so I have booked two."

At last Thom heard the lock as it clicked open, it awoke him. Iyengar returned accompanied by Dino who pulled out the second chair to sit directly opposite Thom and stared intensely into his eyes.

Thom addressed Dino. "I don't know why you are here but now that you are will you please tell this clown to remove these ridiculous handcuffs?"

"Not quite yet, Professor Miller," said Dino in a voice that sounded mildly light-hearted, almost amused. "I am very interested to know why Dimitri found you in a restricted area. Your method of entry was ingenious; however, I think you must have had assistance to create such a sophisticated master key. Perhaps you would like to help me with these matters so that I understand. I know a great deal about you, but not why you went to so much trouble to trespass somewhere you were never meant to visit."

Thom resisted the urge to vent the anger that had

been growing. He recognised that he was at a serious disadvantage and he detected something deep and malevolent lurking beneath Dino's supercilious light-heartedness. Better not to provoke him, he decided. He said:

"Perhaps you will tell me what is going on here?"

Looking straight into Thom's eyes Dino asked, "Have you not used your considerable skills of analysis to work out what is taking place? I have heard so much about the very clever professor to whom I owe a great debt of gratitude, for you have solved the last remaining problem and unlocked the secret of M2. You have ensured that we can go into production within days and then I shall become one of the richest, most powerful men in the world. I owe this in part to you and for which you have my heartfelt thanks."

Thom stared straight back at Dino and said, "It's the hormone isn't it? M2 will only work with hormones extracted from humans. I suspect that it is gender-specific also."

"Wonderful Professor, I thought you would get there. Does my little farm offend your sensibilities?"

"If I have anything to do with it you will be dragged through the courts and spend the rest of your life in jail. These poor innocents have been deprived of their lives so that you can accumulate wealth and power, it is the single most abhorrent act I have ever come across."

"Now, now, Professor, let's not be sentimental. Their lives were worthless. They were refugees who probably would have drowned in the Mediterranean, and even if they had survived most would have been destined to return home to die in the same poverty and in the same country from where they sought to escape. In fact, the countries from which they struggle to leave have so little regard for the lives of their citizens that these people, for whom you show such touching concern, are often killed without compunction. Either it is tribal war or human trafficking, such men have not a jot of humanity and those in the west care even less despite their posturing. There are millions amongst the diaspora whose useless lives are pointless. They are of no more significance than the insects you and I casually crush beneath our shoe. The western world pretends to care but makes no more effort to save them than we would to help ants. These people die every day and no nation does anything much to assist because the lives of refugees don't matter. Perhaps some do-gooders care but most people turn the page of their breakfast newspaper and spread their jam. My 'children' are the displaced, the dispossessed and the meaningless. I at least give some purpose to their birth.

"Professor," Dino continued, "you espouse the sanctimonious liberal sensibilities of the western world, but like the rest of your kind you don't care enough to make a difference. People die every day from illegal drugs or they are trafficked for prostitution and, believe me, much worse. What for? For the money and power of those who strive to accumulate ever greater amounts of money and power. Is any effective action ever taken to stop them? No. And the reason is that those who don't have either money or power are impotent. Those who want to bring about change don't because they are too busy passing laws to enshrine universal rights and in so doing they emasculate their own authority. Conclusion, Professor?

The only meaningful influence comes from the accumulation of wealth and power, but to be wealthy and powerful one must be ruthless. So the compassionate society in which you believe so fervently is not only a misnomer it is pure sophistry. My creed, I can assure you, will always trump yours."

Thom responded, "You are despicable. Care and compassion distinguish us from animals and you espouse neither."

In a cold fury Dino snarled, "Well let me tell you something else. When M2 hits the market and those who can afford it are able to live appreciably longer, most of them won't give a damn about its provenance, there will be no price too high, fiscal or moral, to pay for their longevity."

"God help your soul," said Thom.

"Oh, what makes you think I have one? That is your belief, not mine," flashed Dino.

Thom's riposte was instantaneous. "You and your kind are pure evil. You cause destruction, exploitation and corrosion of everything worthwhile. You value nothing except for its material worth, you exist only for your own perverted greed. Fortunately, though, there are those who believe in equality and justice. The battle between the noble and the savage continues and we know which defines you, Dino."

"Perhaps if I look beyond the stars I will find God," replied Dino artfully.

The full meaning of Dino's words suddenly struck Thom and it was as if he had been administered with a high ampage electric shock. He sat bolt upright. "You have no concept of God; why do you mention seeing through stars to find the good in the world?"

"Well," said Dino, "I have heard the expression used so often in the last two years."

"Why choose that phrase?" said Thom, holding his breath.

"Do you honestly think that I am so casual about my possessions that I would allow someone to adulterate something pure that belongs to me? Of course I have known about you and Ariadne from the very start in London. The two of you have been observed at almost every moment and recorded whenever you were together. There is very little I have not seen and heard and it has disgusted me.

"You should understand that I have planned carefully how to draw you into my web, it is why you were invited to Athens. I wanted you here in Crete so that I could exact the appropriate retribution."

In a flash of intuition Thom understood the full scope of Dino's sociopathic nature. "Angela and…?"

"Exactly. I fear so," said Dino with a thin smile. "And poor Little Tom."

"I was wrong, you are not a savage, you are a beast."

At last Dino was provoked. With clenched cheeks and a sneer in his voice he coolly replied to Thom.

"So is this what happens to the man of logic and cold, hard reason when he meets a romantic? She diminishes him with quixotic notions and mystical poetry. He is emasculated by ideas rather than facts and absolutes. She reduces the man of science to an intellectual pygmy, one who starts to live with fairy tales of gods and philosophies of goodwill, of right and wrong, she even talks to him of a spiritual redeemer. Well, let me tell you she is no different from her ancient Greek ancestors. They made deals with their gods in the hope of appeasing them and to gain protection from the powerful, ruthless men and forces of nature that bring destruction. Well her gods won't and can't protect her because I shall have my revenge for the injustice she has done to me. She could have chosen me, I would have given her wealth and power, instead she wanted you, a liar and cheat who betrayed his wife and child and stole my wife. I despise you, Thomas Miller."

In a weary voice Thom replied, "You are so full of hatred that you have become indifferent to the value of life, but human history has shown time and again that those who uphold humanity triumph in the end. You will be held to account, take my word for it."

As Thom was talking Dino made a sign to Iyengar who had been standing to one side and who now moved across behind him to slip a belt over Thom's head and down to his chest, trapping his upper arms against the chair. At the same moment Dino reached forward and deliberately rolled Thom's shirt sleeve up above his elbow. Iyengar handed Dino a syringe filled with a clear liquid. Dino held it up and pushed gently against the plunger until a small bead of fluid emerged and glistened in the light. He leaned forward and with all the irony he could muster said, "A small scratch, Professor," as he slid the needle into Thom's vein.

As the anaesthetic began to take effect Thom's final words were slurred, "You are truly a monster."

PART THIRTEEN

Minotaur

Ariadne and Aristotle caught the 18.30 Olympic Airlines flight from Athens to Heraklion. The company jet was still unavailable and their only option was a scheduled flight. Such was their sense of urgency that they had immediately booked seats, and travelled lightly with only cabin baggage.

Before departing Athens, Aristotle had to rearrange his diary and he wanted to explain to Martha why he was rushing off so urgently. He did not share the detail concerning his sudden decision, but enough to leave her nervous and concerned for what he intended to do on Crete.

The flight touched down on time. Ariadne had left the Land Cruiser in the airport car park and so their journey through the relatively small terminal was quickly expedited and by ten o'clock that evening they were approaching Plati, having driven at speed across the island. As they approached the house Ariadne sought desperately for signs of Thom's presence, but there were no lights showing and the Land Rover was not parked in the drive; it seemed clear that he was not at home. Despite numerous attempts she was still unable to reach him on his mobile phone and the litany of messages she had left on his voicemail remained unanswered. Her anxiety level was high and increasing all the time.

Once inside the house she established quickly that there was no message from Thom, either written or on the answerphone. She had heard nothing more from him since his text of 18.45 informing her that he was going to explore the labyrinth. She had not received the text until nearly an hour later after they had landed and she switched on her phone.

Ariadne wanted to go straight to Lasithi and search for Thom, but Aristotle asserted his authority and insisted they wait for the morning.

"We cannot go barging onto the site when we don't have a plan of action. It will be natural for us to be there in the morning and we can execute a search without causing too much disruption. More importantly we shall need help and I have someone who can assist, but I shall have to explain what is required and why. Dino is a dangerous man and the two of us cannot overcome him alone. Please, Ariadne, be guided by me."

"If Thom is in danger then we must go now and help him, we might save his life. You can call upon the security people to help."

"No. I'm sorry. We will find Thom in the morning, but I won't agree to precipitous action. There is a great deal at stake here which I can resolve as long as we contain the situation. You must be guided by me."

Reluctantly she agreed and they headed for their respective bedrooms, Aristotle opting for the suite he had always favoured when the family were together all those many years before.

Ariadne could not sleep. She tossed, turned and when occasionally she was about to slip over the edge into sleep, images of Thom flashed across her semi-conscious mind bringing her fully awake again. Somewhere in the early hours of the morning she tried to analyse in what ways Thom had come to dominate her very existence. No, dominate was the wrong word, he had come to complement her life. It was as if she were only whole when near him. It was far more than just his physical presence, it was the recognition that she defined herself as part of him, there was no longer a me, only an us. She could operate independently, but she was only ever fully affirmed when a part of the whole, and this was when they occupied the same physical orbit. They were each a subset of the one, together they created the whole and then they were complete.

Life without Thom would be unthinkable for she would be torn apart from her spiritual counterpart. God had given him to her and together in their love she believed they were made in God's image. She had been graced by God's divine love.

She slept fitfully for a couple of hours until dawn arrived and when she awoke she was tired and experiencing such a sense of lassitude that for a few moments she wondered if she were paralysed.

When Ariadne and Aristotle reached the office Nikki had just arrived at her desk to prepare for the day. She was shocked to see how emotionally ravaged her boss appeared. Ariadne explained that she was not to be disturbed and Nikki was perfectly content to take control of the office to free father and daughter for the day. She was delighted to meet Aristotle again for she had a soft spot for the older man, but it was clear that something was seriously out of kilter.

"Have you seen anything of Professor Miller since I left?" asked Ariadne.

"No, sadly not," was the light-hearted reply, possibly rather too flippant she concluded by the look on Ariadne's face.

As soon as Nikki had closed the door Ariadne said, "We must go and search Thom's office." As she turned to leave the room Aristotle was surprised to see her pick up a torch. It was some distance to the physics laboratories and Engelmann was taken aback to see them barging into the department and heading straight for Thom's study. They ignored him.

Once safely inside Ariadne drew the blinds and explained to Aristotle, "We had an agreement that we would keep a log of our clandestine activities written in ultraviolet ink, hence the UV torch. The diary is in the bottom drawer of his desk."

Aristotle opened the third drawer and sure enough the log book was safely there. The final entry had been written the previous day noting that all the senior staff were away and Thom was going to investigate what lay behind the movable cupboard in the operating theatre.

"OK said Aristotle. We cannot go blundering through the operating theatre while all the staff are working. You are just going to have to contain yourself until after the end of work today."

"No. Surely not? Let off a fire alarm, do something, we have to go and look."

"I'm sorry, this time you will have to do what you are told. Come with me, there is someone we must see."

Ariadne followed Aristotle along numerous passageways and was surprised at how well he knew his way around, but then she recalled that he had designed this labyrinth of tunnels, they were a part of his kingdom.

When Aristotle came to a halt it was outside the office of Georges Papadopolus. Aristotle knocked and walked straight in.

"Welcome, my old friend," said Georges, rising

from his chair and coming over to give Aristotle a fraternal hug. It was obvious they knew each other well. "Welcome also Mrs Minas, what can I do for you both?"

"I will get straight to it, Georges. For a long time, you have been my eyes here at Lasithi and I have been grateful for all your reports. Indeed, just recently you alerted me to the nocturnal visit of my daughter to this office."

Ariadne looked abashed.

"Now I have need of your help again. You have reported incongruous events and shared with me your concern that something intangible is taking place, well you are right, but now something has transpired that makes matters a whole lot more serious. Professor Miller has gone missing, disappeared off the face of the earth here in our buildings. We believe your last sighting would be yesterday evening at about 18.25. Can you trace his movements for us?"

Without hesitation Georges set about the task and within a relatively short period of time was able to confirm that Thom had entered the area of Bio-technology at 18.35 the previous evening.

"I am running a face recognition scan to see when he returned but can't seem to find a record of him leaving Bio-tech. I will search to see who else may have visited yesterday evening."

"I have a further requirement," said Aristotle. "This evening I want you to become blind in the areas I have listed for you." He handed over a piece of paper. "I will inform you when everything may be returned to normal but this evening I need you to

245

keep a watch for me and if there is any activity in the Bio-tech area you must alert me with this bleeper. I ask a lot but this is of the greatest importance and highest priority."

"My dear friend, you know that you can rely upon me absolutely."

The rest of that day was an agony for Ariadne. In the middle of the afternoon Aristotle informed her that there was a task he had to undertake and he left her alone to fret and worry even further. Her concern for Thom had settled into a deep, pervasive fear. He had been absent too long.

Finally, the end of the working day approached. Georges Papadopolus had sent a memo around to all staff informing them that there was to be a security lockdown that evening at 18.00 hours and everyone was to leave the premises prior to that time. This included all security guards who were to congregate in the guardroom at the main entrance until informed they may return to their stations.

Soon after six o'clock there was an eerie silence in the buildings and at quarter past six Ariadne and Aristotle were ready to begin their search. She felt nauseous and was experiencing a headache that could only be compared with a belt being gradually tightened around her skull. She collected her torch, which she informed Aristotle would lead them to Thom if he were lost in unknown underground tunnels. He would have marked his route with the invisible substance highlighted by ultraviolet.

They reached the operating theatre without incident and rapidly established the layout. The cupboard was where Thom had reported it to be and they had no difficulty sliding it to one side. Ariadne shone her torch and sure enough painted on the door behind was a large X shape illuminated by the ultraviolet beam of light.

Entry into the short corridor behind was straightforward, as was the summoning of and descent in the lift. The locked door that lay ahead was once again marked with an X. As they approached Ariadne reached for her father's hand and slipped hers into his as easily and naturally as she had when she was six years old. Aristotle passed his card across the security pad and entered his pin before presenting his thumb. They waited a moment until there was a click and with a gentle push the door swung open.

The first thing to attract Ariadne's attention was a table straight ahead of her separating two chairs that faced each other. On one chair was a pair of handcuffs attached by a chain to the wall behind. She felt her father's hand tighten on hers and when she looked up she was unprepared for the sight that faced her, serried ranks of what looked like frozen people hanging from the ceiling.

"Now I understand," said Aristotle.

Ariadne went forward to look at the first row and said, "Oh my god, there are people inside these coffins. Are they alive?"

"Not in the way that you and I think of being alive."

She walked along the front row and then looked to the right where three other mannequin shapes were hanging. She could see that two were empty but the third was occupied. She stepped forward to look more closely. Her father caught her just before she collapsed to the floor.

Aristotle carried Ariadne and sat her in one of the chairs where there was a half empty bottle of water that he shook into her face until she started to come round. She took one look at her father and then her face seemed to fall apart as memory flooded back.

"Is he dead?"

"Yes, I'm afraid so. Or at least he is dead to you although his body continues to function. He cannot be brought back." At that moment there was a low whistle from the beeper in Aristotle's pocket. He stood, squared his shoulders and faced the door. He waited for the lock to click open.

"Come in Dino," Aristotle said.

"Splendid. Splendid," said Dino as he entered. "I have been anticipating this meeting for a long time."

"Why, Dino? Why Thom?" whispered Ariadne.

"But you know the answer to that, my dear, you surely don't need me to spell everything out. When I first found out about your torrid little affair I was so angry that you had betrayed me I wanted you dead. I called upon the services of a company I know, but something went wrong and Petra got in the way. Then as your adultery became ever more flagrant I decided you deserved a much more severe punishment. I would deprive you of everything you thought you wanted. Well, here we are and the time has come."

As he had been talking, Dino walked up to Thom's suit and looked through the glass before giving it a long kiss at mouth height. Ariadne shuddered.

"Tell me Dino," said Aristotle, "were you involved in Andro's death?"

Turning to answer as he paced around the room he gave his answer. "Ah yes, that was so tragic, wasn't it? But the thing is, and you won't believe me, he deserved what happened. He discovered at a very early stage the necessity for human hormone in the production of M2 and he threatened me. He demanded that the research be stopped. What we were achieving was far too important for anyone to be allowed to call a halt, especially the spoiled brat that was Andro."

"So you killed your brother and nearly broke your mother's heart."

"Correction. He was not my natural brother and it was my mother's back that was broken when I pushed her down that ridiculous staircase you built. She tried to thwart me and insisted that I should divorce you, Ariadne."

"Good God," said Aristotle.

"Oh don't talk to me about God," replied Dino. "Keep that nonsense for her. She is the simpleton who yearns for a mystical union. Of course God might appear in a moment to save you, but I rather doubt it."

Dino turned to Ariadne. "I chose you. I gave you the opportunity to enjoy unimaginable wealth and power and what did you do? You spurned me and chose instead to cavort with that sentimental fool of a physicist. He filled your head with all sorts of notions and nonsense. You can't do that, Ariadne, and get away with it unpunished.

"When M2 comes into production I shall be one of the richest men on Earth. The influential and powerful of the world will seek me out and I shall guide their actions."

"And what is your vision for the world?" asked Aristotle quietly.

"We will create a ruling elite selected by wealth and power alone. As for the rest I really don't give a damn. As long as they are quiescent they will be allowed to live useful but meaningless lives: corruption and greed will flourish among those not under our protection and we shall exploit their activities.

"One thing I can tell you is that poetry will not occupy a special place, nor will your God, Ariadne. The elite will live a long time and those who subscribe to our vision will be allowed to extend their natural life by many years, the others will not. I am prepared to bet that most people will accept the deal that offers extended life, even if they find some of my conditions unpalatable."

"And what about us? Are we going to live a long time, Dino?" enquired Aristotle.

"Oh no, I am afraid not, that's why there are two empty suits hanging here. Ariadne you will be with Thom soon. I have some papers here, Aristotle, that I need you to sign. Doctor Iyengar is outside the door. He has a loaded pistol although I am not anticipating he will have to use it unless you are uncompliant, in which case he will shoot Ariadne in the extremities until you do as I instruct. After that, well your future offers the opportunity to do something worthwhile for mankind."

"But Dino," said Aristotle, seeming to swell with authority, "that is not what is going to happen. If you take a look outside the door you will see that Doctor Iyengar is under armed guard."

The colour drained from Dino's face and he looked around confused before opening the door to confirm what Aristotle had said. Shock and anger was his response at the sight of the doctor handcuffed and trembling with fear.

"You can't do this. We are on the brink of making the most important contribution to world health ever. We will transform society."

"No. These poor, benighted people will be taken from here and given a suitable burial according to their belief. Every trace of M2 and its existence will be destroyed so that no one can ever reproduce what you have created. In you I have created a monster, Dino."

"But you can't stop me. I will start again. It was I who created this great revolution and no one can obstruct me wherever you might try to hide me away."

"I was concerned that you would say that."

"Are you threatening me?" screamed Dino. "I am

your son. You would not do anything to hurt me."

"You are right, Dino. I would not do anything to hurt my son, you murdered him, but as you observed a few moments ago you are not my natural son. Sit down, Dino, and listen to me. Are you capable of repentance? Can you understand that you have offended against man and God?"

"Oh don't be so ridiculous Aristotle, you sound like one of those ancient Greeks Ariadne is always going on about," spluttered Dino.

"Which is exactly my point," said Aristotle, "I am one of those ancient Greeks and you have offended against the gods, which, if you study your literature you will know cannot be tolerated. Your act of outrageous hubris brings with it inevitable nemesis."

As he spoke Aristotle was moving around the room and very carefully he withdrew from his pocket a small phial. When he was standing directly behind Dino he pulled out the stopper extremely gently, attached to which was a fine needle, rather like those used for acupuncture. As Aristotle passed in front of Dino he casually scraped the needle across the skin of Dino's left hand, just above the fingers, causing him to bleed slightly.

"What was that?" shouted Dino.

"I am sorry, Dino, but over the next five minutes you will discover that I have just injected you with a drop of tetanospasmin, a toxin that I removed from Section 31 this afternoon. Because of your scientific background you will know that it only requires a tenth of a milligram to be fatal and you have ingested more than that. The botulism interferes with the nervous system, messing up certain neurotransmitters and causing muscle spasm. You will soon begin to experience difficulty breathing, your jaw will lock, your back will arch and then you will be racked by uncontrollable paroxysms. You will lose control of your bowels and bladder and I apologise in advance, but you will experience terrible pain before death. Ariadne, my dear you might wish to leave the room."

"No, Father," she replied, "I will stay until the very end."

Ariadne was sitting on the sofa. She put aside the piece of paper upon which she had copied the first verse of John Donne's *Nocturnal Upon St Lucy's Day*[12].

> *It is the year's midnight, and it is the day's,*
>
> *Lucy's, who scarce seven hours herself unmasks;*
>
> *The sun is spent, and now his flasks*
>
> *Send forth light squibs, no constant rays;*
>
> *The world's whole sap is sunk;*
>
> *The general balm th' hydroptic earth hath drunk,*
>
> *Whither, as to the bed's-feet, life is shrunk*[13]*.*

---

[12] *St Lucy's Day* is the shortest day of the year
[13] '*Nocturnal Upon St Lucy's Day*' – see Part 15 for the whole poem

In contrast to the mid-winter of the poem she was reading that morning there were signs of spring outside. Ariadne looked through the panoramic window of the house at Plati and beyond where she could see the signs of warmth awakening the countryside and creeping across the hillsides that were covered with vigorous, verdant growth. Everywhere there were signs of renewal, life revisiting the world, heralding Persephone's return. The colourful beehives that decorated the hills around the plateau stood out in striking contrast to the dark earth, and the olive groves were swarming with apian activity. The scent of natural herbs, growing so pungently on the hillside, was, she knew, pervasive in the early morning dew and the cataracts that had dispersed the melting snow were reducing to a trickle, drying with the promise of summer. As she looked up the sun burst over the top of the mountain full of exuberance, the harbinger of new life. But she was numb, her life shrunken as if to the bed's feet.

Following the truly awful events of the previous day her father had taken control. The authorities had been called and delicate negotiation had followed. It was in no one's interest for the facts around the events at Lasithi to become known publicly. The 'bodies' had been disconnected and removed discreetly.

Aristotle had explained to her that Section 31 was a highly secret joint collaboration between Minas Industries and the Greek government investigating the most dangerous diseases known to man. Dino's body had been found in one of the laboratories of Section 31 and the authorities concluded that he must have accidentally scratched himself when working with a deadly toxin. After much deliberation Ariadne agreed that Thom was to be returned to his parents in England to be interred near Angela and Little Tom. Engelmann had been ignorant of the activities below ground, but Doctors Iyengar and Wójcik were arrested and would be quietly incarcerated in a place from where they would never emerge to inform the world of the ground-breaking development of M2. M2 would be quietly forgotten, another development with great promise that proved to be a false dawn.

A false dawn, Ariadne thought. *But for me there will be no dawn at all.* In her more floridly romantic moments she had imagined they were immortal, they might one day come to embody the couple who united the panoply of reason and emotion perfectly matched. Perhaps a constellation would be named after them, like Castor and Pollux, but now she could only immortalise Thom through her words, her poems, it would be her life's vocation.

They had not been immortal; they had been ripped apart by an evil beast that stalked the earth. All that she had dreamed of, all that she had loved and all that she had come to believe would be her future had been shattered and she felt hopeless. What remained were her memories and the knowledge of the love she held for him, and that alone would last for it was infinite and enduring, it was perpetual, it was her little piece of God.

Epilogue

Ariadne had sat at the mouth of the cave for three beginnings and three ends of the day. Virtually without moving she had held tight to the end of the string in the knowledge that Theseus would return to her.

There was a twitch upon the thread.

Nearby sat her namesake, also under an ancient olive tree centuries old. They were separated by a few yards and millennia. On her lap was a notebook and in her hand a pen. A large straw hat helped preserve her perfect complexion and at her side lay an open picnic basket.

An observer would have noted a woman in her sixth decade, still youthful and with an aura of serenity that emphasised her beauty, although behind her was cast a shadow of sadness.

Tucked into the basket was a manuscript and had it been possible to see the title then the subject might have made obvious the content, especially to one who knew her story, *'Lifelonging'*.

With a look of complete concentration and focus she began to compose once again.

RUCKSACK

Ageing, although not yet ancient, I am conscious of the weight
Reducing. From time to time I unpack a few of those gems,
The jewels that have been accumulated and catalogued.
Some sparkle still, others have dulled, and there are those with
Jagged edges capable of inflicting hurt, even at this distance.
I realise that some are lost, they leech away; the crush
Will be eased as the repository gradually diminishes.

I hold one to my ear and it resonates with my mother's laughter
But louder is the surf that laps at the shore of my being, lit by
his smile.
Another glistens with ice and November mist among Oxford
spires.
Hands entwined and souls set free to soar, we stride the
Universe undaunted.
Darker ones
When sorrow drowns my happiness in tears.

A wedding dress and the laughter of children, holidays on the
strand
And journeys through the Loire with a man whose heart is
gladly and
Gently given, he is my balm and redemption from the mire.

I cradle these memories and carefully repack the rucksack,
Knowing that the ones I dare not remove are at the centre
And shine most brightly, all others made dim.

Night has fallen as she places her pen upon her lap and looks up to the sky where the stars shine as though through a blanket, one she would like to wrap around her shoulders. But her gaze does not stop at the stars and passes far beyond. Under her breath she whispers, "God bless you, Thom."

PART FOURTEEN

Lifelonging

Ariadne Minas

Dedicated to the memory of Thomas Miller

'This weak and idle theme, no more yielding but a dream'

INAMORATA

At least I can turn the bloody tele off,
But your image persists.
Present tensed, a timed bomb, ticking.
No! Not ready to explode, but implode,
Turn upon itself. "Where the hell's the Valium?"

This drama is incomplete. A happy ending? I wonder.
Pent up, sick at times, hollow inside — longing —
Eternally yearning.

Each day when I awake
You materialise, the picture crystal clear,
Smiling, laughing, mercilessly appealing. Silently
Calling to me, always trapped, just out of reach
Within the cathode tube of my mind. Tragedy? Comedy?
Farce? Which scenario is being played today? The
Characters never change, only the scenes.

Sometimes you catch me out, like the ads. You
Cut into my thoughts, my day dreams, my being.
You dominate the action, then slide away only to reappear,
Unexpected, a few minutes later.

Dreams. Is there no escape?

Where's the remote control? Rewind. Why the hell

Doesn't the fast forward work? Hit the pause button.

Oh how I long, how I ache, how I crave when we are apart.

At night, as sleep encroaches, your image is the dying impression…

Receding… sleep, the certain knot of peace… but not.

Blank screen…enter subconscious stage right…

TESSERAE

Patterns pound relentlessly upon the retina of my imagination,
Shifting, sliding like tectonic plates upon the mantle of thoughts;
Images as permanent as prints in sand are lapped by memories
Eddying, swirling, waxing, waning, silent and vivid.

But at the still point of my kaleidoscopic mind
There a liquid centre hardens, crystallises
And defines, what? You who do not slip away into
Hazy recollection but stand sharply defined.

Patterns, an endless succession of spectres who always
Knock, enter and demand attention. Tessellated
Images and thoughts from the core of my being.
In half light, vivid and indistinct they creep from a
Montage past to dictate future action.

But now, unbidden, memories and thoughts of you are constant,
Like a pulse. Others come, go, gossip of Michael and Angelo,
But you recur as a theme, a melody, a roundel, like Pachelbel –
I dwell on nothing else.

The fecundity of my imagination follows a
Pattern but returns to that shape which now
Shapes the patterns of my thoughts…

As I lie by the fire the images of my mind recede,
They look on, but to us they must concede.

BEGINNINGS

A student bar and fervent clamour of restless youth; time held at bay. The

Desire is instant, loud and defiant, irreconcilable with the hands of the clock.

And as the day dissolves and passion resounds, the Spinner of the Years calls

Time for the two whose immortality is imminent, to be razed up among the gods.

Later, knowing and hoping, I climb the oak and look to the horizon,

Watching for a sail, some small encouragement to promote hope, hope

Like acid burning.

In Oxford the coals shimmer in the heat when chance and circumstance

Conspire alone, and an intricate tapestry is woven in the stars.

A kiss.

A kiss that burns as a candle lit at both ends,

Before we give flight to our heels and we flee.

Exhilaration.

The screw is tightened, the Minotaur lurks in the

Shadows as the sail is raised and

A sacrifice is promised.

IN THE ROOM

(Him – from notes found in TM's diary)

The first time I saw you a door opened and a clock stopped.
A single moment, suspended.

As when Paris took his first step toward Troy, or when
Charles Ryder's small opening in an Oxford wall was revealed,
I entered, and my Helen approached, calm and statuesque,
hand extended,
Sculpted in porcelain, chiselled ankles, perpendicular poise,
Perfect proportion.

A glimpse, as of Emily, and there would be no further peace.
Incoherence, an epiphany on the road to my Damascus, and
The compass swung. There was a tilt, the axis realigned and,
As for Oedipus pegged on a hill,
A course was plotted.

From that moment until my last breath we alone would be
together,
Somewhere. My sylvan Muse, spoke, smiled and dazzled
While the Eumenides watched through a window and
Nodded at what would be.

IN THE WOODS

Autumn and dusk encroaches as the two who would be one approach their

Eden, aware that one step further taken will be to enter a kingdom, the realm of

Angels, the searing exultation of God's embrace, their apotheosis, the immutable

Coincidence of their nativity.

Poised at the threshold, innocence nearly shed, an imminent fusion of immortality.

What happens next is confused. Eyes locked, and beyond words they falter clumsily

As the gate to Paradise both opens and shuts.

Unaware of place or time as the angels look on through the bars,

Sadness in their blessing at this communion, God's purpose is

Fulfilled in a declaration and consummation, a spark from the

Perpetual fire and eternal peace denied thereafter.

Darkness and the mist creep into the chapel as the two emerge to part,

Bound upon the wheel, stumbling toward and away from the consuming fire.

The Furies head for home, satisfied.

MESSIAH

(Innocence)

The music soared into the ark of the nave
As we sat, a covenant of another kind, enshrined;
A chorus of singers, and our fingers intertwined.

Jeremy sang on a damp, cold, November evening while
The warmth of our love flowed from a hidden door, pure,
Where joy issued; never before so sure, entire and secure.

We came heavy laden, the world poised to traduce,
But were redeemed as the trumpet sounded; unbound
And surrounded, the glory of the Lord seemed to resound.

For a fleeting, enchanted, moment we were raised up incorruptible,

Suspended for a few beats, and in the heat of our love we believed

He perceived, His purpose in our own Amen lovingly received.

I LOVE YOU

Three words,
inconsequential,
but

By you uttered,
the progenitor
of a Super Nova,

Engender in me
an explosion of
cosmic proportion.

What matters coils
into a density,
a mass unsustainable

Triggered by those words
That grant me
supremacy

To roam the heavens,
a celestial king
newly born.

(TM)

THE NATURE OF LOVE

Like lovers clasped in irons the planets and time
Bind each close with captive band, adamantine.
From north to south, like magnets to the poles,
Earth and Moon dance intricate steps, souls,
Locked like atoms in an embrace that can't be broken,
Are bound apart in one another's arms, love unspoken.
Held by a force stronger than their nativity
Endlessly, orbiting in the other's gravity.

So the nature of love and the lover imitate the stars' passion;
Cannot draw apart, fused and compelled by their attraction,
They form a universal perfection, bound in perpetual motion.
And, as it is that we perceive an object in its reflection,
Your love is mirrored by the devotion you see in me,
Which is the compulsion of love, the love I feel for thee.

(TM)

OXFORD

Those ancient stones, were they impassive or did they in judgement sit?

Perhaps, warmed by love and Albinoni seeping into their cold façade, did

They turn their gaze toward the brief joy within where two hearts beat?

Or perhaps, ascetic in judgement, did they recoil recalling Newman

In his apostolic, austere Oxford bed, whose cold and sinless disapprobation

Was transcended by the absorption, the fire that raged within those walls?

Maybe as an angel passed, a tear was shed
For the flame that burned and consumed
The two who were as one, incandescent.

Or perhaps the serpent celebrated a victory as I feared,
The voice of childhood binding me tight, the penance of a sinner,
Not as a celebrant on the altar of our bed but a sacrifice.

There again, it is just possible that in the presence of such passion
And love, Newman's stones smiled and offered a benediction
As two became one and the moon shone brightly around the mullion.

THE PARTING

*Centuries to grow, how does an ancient tree feel when the
final blow of the axe parts it from its roots?*

*When I told him
I cried*

*Something broke
Inside*

*The door to the fourth dimension
Closed*

*Our love was forever I
Supposed*

*But the glass cage in which our love was
forged*

*Shattered - a small shard cut a brilliant
cord*

*And, drowning, you slipped from my grip
deep*

*A mortal wound and still I
Weep*

MESSIAH

(Experience)

It was dark, a mist surrounded the
Church

And the frost sparkled. The air sounded a
Bell

In the distance there was an arterial
Rumble

As we sat in the nave joined as two in a
Womb

Twins absorbed by the Messiah which about us
Soared

Light, false hope, an all-consuming love
Before

A still birth and a return to the night and
Dark

REFLECTION

I know the hours for I have relived them all; a few glorious months,

But how many were we together alone? The razor blade moments

where we carved our happiness are vivid and if traded would have a

Value greater than a splinter from the cross. Faustus chose amiss;

Every kiss, touch, look, glance, stolen moment, caress - they survive as bliss.

Together as one in mind spirit and soul, free and without hesitation

In our capitulation, we rose like eagles upon the wind and soared, regal,

All thereafter would be rapture captured and distilled without equal.

Every small velvet curve and crease of your body vibrant still;

Moments sensual as a clock's spring wound tight to breaking.

But I can't recall how often we made love as the hour shrank,

Only the sublime essence, the ascent, the pinnacle of all fruition

Released, as if Adam with Eve came again in passionate union.

I ask again what was our allotted slot? A slice of a lifetime in which

All seemed revealed but remained concealed; a sealed tomb where we

Resided triumphant for a while, blinded by a future we could not see.

CONFUSION

From where did that passion find expression?
His hand guided furiously, November fire fuelled by that single
Night and the hope it sparked?

His words transcending meaning, transmuting. Each a droplet,
An essence - the potion, an elixir, an alchemy distilled;
Not in base materials, but stirred in my soul. My soul bared.
A whisper of laughter beyond the pane.

Just perhaps an ordination, the sail set for
Byzantium, but can the centre hold?
I topple in indecision.

Agonies of the irresolute as the world inexorably turns,
Doomed to live with silence that aches and burns.
A nightingale in a golden cage singing with none to hear?
A rustling of wings behind the curtain and a burden to bear.

TOGETHER AND APART

For her:

Squalls gather on the horizon that grow and advance
To slowly drown future joy. The gates to arcadia begin to close
And on either side she views a void deep and bleak.

And as the dream begins to break she sees them tossed toward
A shore, she glimpses their wreckage burgeoning.

For him:

A sight, a glance, an anticipation, and adrenaline spurts as copiously
As before - and as dusk approaches the candle burns more brightly -
But "why, why, did he submit to Shakespearean hours and let tragedy
Unfold"?

For them:

The children of the storms will be gradually overwhelmed,
As slowly they are drawn deeper into the labyrinth until
The string drops and terrors of the darkness lie ahead.

AFTERWARDS

The Eumenides have grown old and tired, their passions nearly spent, the

Pursuit less eager and weary of the chase, they have set sail.

And

If I could hold up a glass would I see my longing mirrored across the years

Returning from each visit to the shrine with memories seared

Onto life-long silver nitrate that blurs, we were together when

I was so, so alone.

But is it

A tragedy, unable to belong lifelong - a sacrifice, a penance to atone?

And

I cannot help and wonder if with time, would I have diminished and

Trod the road on my own?

Those furies, embers now, amused by the Muses, entertained by our dalliance,

Look elsewhere for semblance and as the years slip away, the brilliance diminishing,

But that great question reverberates.

MICHAEL SPINNEY

IN MEMORIAM

(Mistaken)

The church was crowded, a memorial to a time
And place from whence once came my help,
An influence benign and in my beginning.
As we remembered I glanced across the room and
Time froze as all those years ago. You looked up and smiled,
Your serene beauty radiant and radiating, struck me,
Undiminished by decades. Transfixed I am now
Pinned again by the devotion so hard suppressed, and
Reminded of a passion only extinguished by my end -
Through which lies the hope of resurrection
And yearning for a beginning.

BETTER

To have loved and lost comes at a cost.
Better not at all, but that's a call
I could not make, even for the Almighty's sake.
Never since has He granted me a glimpse
Of that which lies behind the veil, only in our tale,
Where all beauty He creates was manifest in your grace,
His deeper purpose now clear, you are close and near
Ever present, hidden in all that is bidden.

MICHAEL SPINNEY

RUCKSACK

Ageing, although not yet ancient, I am conscious of the weight
Reducing. From time to time I unpack a few of those gems,
The jewels that have been accumulated and catalogued.
Some sparkle still, others have dulled, and there are those with
Jagged edges capable of inflicting hurt, even at this distance.
I realise that some are lost, they leech away; the crush
Will be eased as the repository gradually diminishes.

I hold one to my ear and it resonates with my mother's laughter
But louder is the surf that laps at the shore of my being, lit by
his smile.
Another glistens with ice and November mist among Oxford
spires.
Hands entwined and souls set free to soar, we stride the
Universe undaunted.
Darker ones
When sorrow drowns my happiness in tears.

A wedding dress and the laughter of children, holidays on the
strand
And journeys through the Loire with a man whose heart is
gladly and
Gently given, he is my balm and redemption from the mire.

I cradle these memories and carefully repack the rucksack,
Knowing that the ones I dare not remove are at the centre
And shine most brightly, all others made dim.

'Perchance to dream, ay there's the rub'

PART FIFTEEN

References

THE SECOND COMING

Turning and turning in the widening gyre
The falcon cannot hear the falconer;
Things fall apart; the centre cannot hold;
Mere anarchy is loosed upon the world,
The blood-dimmed tide is loosed, and everywhere
The ceremony of innocence is drowned;
The best lack all conviction, while the worst
Are full of passionate intensity.

Surely some revelation is at hand;

Surely the Second Coming is at hand.
The Second Coming! Hardly are those words out
When a vast image out of Spiritus Mundi
Troubles my sight: somewhere in sands of the desert

A shape with lion body and the head of a man,
A gaze blank and pitiless as the sun,
Is moving its slow thighs, while all about it
Reel shadows of the indignant desert birds.
The darkness drops again; but now I know
That twenty centuries of stony sleep
Were vexed to nightmare by a rocking cradle,
And what rough beast, its hour come round at last,
Slouches towards Bethlehem to be born?

W B Yeats

MUSEE DE BEAUX ARTS

About suffering they were never wrong,
The old Masters: how well they understood
Its human position: how it takes place
While someone else is eating or opening a window or just
walking dully along;
How, when the aged are reverently, passionately waiting
For the miraculous birth, there always must be
Children who did not specially want it to happen, skating
On a pond at the edge of the wood:
They never forgot
That even the dreadful martyrdom must run its course

Anyhow in a corner, some untidy spot
Where the dogs go on with their doggy life and the torturer's
horse
Scratches its innocent behind on a tree.
In Brueghel's Icarus, for instance: how everything turns away
Quite leisurely from the disaster; the ploughman may
Have heard the splash, the forsaken cry,
But for him it was not an important failure; the sun shone
As it had to on the white legs disappearing into the green
Water, and the expensive delicate ship that must have seen
Something amazing, a boy falling out of the sky,
Had somewhere to get to and sailed calmly on.

W H Auden

TO HIS COY MISTRESS

Had we but world enough and time,
This coyness, lady, were no crime.
We would sit down, and think which way
To walk, and pass our long love's day.
Thou by the Indian Ganges' side
Shouldst rubies find; I by the tide
Of Humber would complain. I would
Love you ten years before the flood,
And you should, if you please, refuse
Till the conversion of the Jews.
My vegetable love should grow
Vaster than empires and more slow;
An hundred years should go to praise
Thine eyes, and on thy forehead gaze;
Two hundred to adore each breast,
But thirty thousand to the rest;
An age at least to every part,
And the last age should show your heart.
For, lady, you deserve this state,
Nor would I love at lower rate.
But at my back I always hear
Time's wingèd chariot hurrying near;
And yonder all before us lie

Deserts of vast eternity.
Thy beauty shall no more be found;
Nor, in thy marble vault, shall sound
My echoing song; then worms shall try
That long-preserved virginity,
And your quaint honour turn to dust,
And into ashes all my lust;
The grave's a fine and private place,
But none, I think, do there embrace.
Now therefore, while the youthful hue
Sits on thy skin like morning dew,
And while thy willing soul transpires
At every pore with instant fires,
Now let us sport us while we may,
And now, like amorous birds of prey,
Rather at once our time devour
Than languish in his slow-chapped power.
Let us roll all our strength and all
Our sweetness up into one ball,
And tear our pleasures with rough strife
Through the iron gates of life:
Thus, though we cannot make our sun
Stand still, yet we will make him run.

Andrew Marvell

THE CLOTHS OF HEAVEN

Had I the heaven's embroidered cloths,
Enwrought with golden and silver light,
The blue and the dim and the dark cloths
Of night and light and the half-light;
I would spread the cloths under your feet:
But I, being poor, have only my dreams;
I have spread my dreams under your feet;
Tread softly because you tread on my dreams.

W B Yeats

MICHAEL SPINNEY

LEDA AND THE SWAN

A sudden blow: the great wings beating still
Above the staggering girl, her thighs caressed
By the dark webs, her nape caught in his bill,
He holds her helpless breast upon his breast.

How can those terrified vague fingers push
The feathered glory from her loosening thighs?
And how can body, laid in that white rush,
But feel the strange heart beating where it lies?

A shudder in the loins engenders there
The broken wall, the burning roof and tower
And Agamemnon dead.
Being so caught up,
So mastered by the brute blood of the air,
Did she put on his knowledge with his power
Before the indifferent beak could let her drop?

W B Yeats

SONNET 43 (from 'Sonnets of the Portuguese')

How do I love thee? Let me count the ways.
I love thee to the depth and breadth and height
My soul can reach, when feeling out of sight
For the ends of being and ideal grace.
I love thee to the level of every day's
Most quiet need, by sun and candle-light.
I love thee freely, as men strive for right.
I love thee purely, as they turn from praise.
I love thee with the passion put to use
In my old griefs, and with my childhood's faith.
I love thee with a love I seemed to lose
With my lost saints. I love thee with the breath,
Smiles, tears, of all my life; and, if God choose,
I shall but love thee better after death.

SONNET 13

And wilt thou have me fashion into speech
The love I bear thee, finding words enough,
And hold the torch out, while the winds are rough,
Between our faces, to cast light on each?—
I drop it at thy feet. I cannot teach
My hand to hold my spirit so far off
From myself—me—that I should bring thee proof
In words, of love hid in me out of reach.
Nay, let the silence of my womanhood
Commend my woman-love to thy belief,—
Seeing that I stand unwon, however wooed,
And rend the garment of my life, in brief,
By a most dauntless, voiceless fortitude,
Lest one touch of this heart convey its grief.

Elizabeth Barrett Browning

THE GARDEN OF LOVE

I went to the Garden of Love,
And saw what I never had seen:
A Chapel was built in the midst,
Where I used to play on the green.

And the gates of this Chapel were shut,
And Thou shalt not writ over the door;
So I turn'd to the Garden of Love,
That so many sweet flowers bore.

And I saw it was filled with graves,
And tomb-stones where flowers should be:
And Priests in black gowns, were walking their rounds,
And binding with briars, my joys & desires.

William Blake

A NOCTURNAL UPON ST LUCY'S DAY

'Tis the year's midnight, and it is the day's,
Lucy's, who scarce seven hours herself unmasks;
The sun is spent, and now his flasks
Send forth light squibs, no constant rays;
The world's whole sap is sunk;
The general balm th' hydroptic earth hath drunk,
Whither, as to the bed's feet, life is shrunk,
Dead and interr'd; yet all these seem to laugh,
Compar'd with me, who am their epitaph.

Study me then, you who shall lovers be
At the next world, that is, at the next spring;
For I am every dead thing,
In whom Love wrought new alchemy.
For his art did express
A quintessence even from nothingness,
From dull privations, and lean emptiness;
He ruin'd me, and I am re-begot
Of absence, darkness, death: things which are not.

All others, from all things, draw all that's good,
Life, soul, form, spirit, whence they being have;
I, by Love's limbec, am the grave
Of all that's nothing. Oft a flood
Have we two wept, and so
Drown'd the whole world, us two; oft did we grow
To be two chaoses, when we did show

Care to aught else; and often absences
Withdrew our souls, and made us carcasses.

But I am by her death (which word wrongs her)
Of the first nothing the elixir grown;
Were I a man, that I were one
I needs must know; I should prefer,
If I were any beast,
Some ends, some means; yea plants, yea stones detest,
And love; all, all some properties invest;
If I an ordinary nothing were,
As shadow, a light and body must be here.

But I am none; nor will my sun renew.
You lovers, for whose sake the lesser sun
At this time to the Goat is run
To fetch new lust, and give it you,
Enjoy your summer all;
Since she enjoys her long night's festival,
Let me prepare towards her, and let me call
This hour her vigil, and her eve, since this
Both the year's, and the day's deep midnight is.

John Donne

21056724R00169

Printed in Great Britain
by Amazon